Love is
a time of enchantment:
in it all days are fair and all fields
green. Youth is blest by it,
old age made benign: the eyes of love see
roses blooming in December,
and sunshine through rain. Verily
is the time of true-love
a time of enchantment — and
Oh! how eager is woman
to be bewitched!

Library at Home Service
Community Services
Hounslow Library, CentreSpace
24 Treaty Centre, High Street
Hounslow TW3 1ES

YOUR COMMUNITY
YOUR SERVICES

0	1	2	3	4	5	6	7	8	9
240 980			693		365	806	80 87	658	929
790			6343		685	116		818	659
240			993	6464	685	346		3128	
			943			7406	312		9529
						496	1588		
							12X		
							3457		

P10-L-2061

✓

MASK OF FORTUNE

Dermot, Earl of Heronforth, was much sought after by Regency beauties, so his leading a young seventeen-year-old about town was a surprise to everyone. It was an obligation inherited along with his wealth and title from his brother James, for Bobby was the child of James' friend Robert Blain. But Bobby is not what he expects, and his task is not to be as simple as it appears.

Books by Sally James
in the Ulverscroft Large Print Series:

A CLANDESTINE AFFAIR
MIRANDA OF THE ISLAND

SALLY JAMES

MASK OF FORTUNE

A CLANDESTINE AFFAIR

MIRANDA OF THE ISLAND

new.

Complete and Unabridged

ULVERSCROFT
Leicester

First published in Great Britain in 1978 by
Robert Hale Limited
London

First Large Print Edition
published November 1991

British Library CIP Data

James, Sally, *1934* –
 Mask of fortune. – Large print ed. –
 Ulverscroft large print series: romance
 I. Title
 823.914

 ISBN 0–7089–2537–5

Published by
F. A. Thorpe (Publishing) Ltd.
Anstey, Leicestershire
Set by Words & Graphics Ltd.
Anstey, Leicestershire
Printed and bound in Great Britain by
T. J. Press (Padstow) Ltd., Padstow, Cornwall

1

DERMOT, Earl of Heronforth, lounged negligently in the brocade covered chair. His cravat was loosened and his normally impeccable hair was in considerable disarray from the times he had pushed his long-fingered, shapely hand through it. He was utterly at variance with his habitually elegant appearance. With great deliberation he selected a card from the few he held in his hand and placed it on the others before him on the table.

"I fancy you cannot beat that, George," he remarked with satisfaction.

George Fenton, a fair haired, fresh complexioned man, his own cravat hanging about his neck in loose folds, laughed and triumphantly displayed his own cards. The Earl threw his own hand down in disgust.

"You have the luck of the devil tonight," he declared, rising to fetch a full decanter to replace the empty one that stood between them.

"Lucky at cards, unlucky in love," George commented. "I do not seem to make headway with the Lady Anne."

"I had not thought you a marrying man," the Earl laughed.

"I am not, but I have determined that it would be foolish to let a fortune go begging," his friend replied with a shrug. "How fares your own pursuit of the fair Julietta?"

"Scarce *my* pursuit," the Earl disclaimed lazily.

"Oh, we are well aware that the Earl of Heronforth is a catch of the first water, and every unmarried female sets her cap at you," his companion rejoined with a laugh. "But I had thought you were not averse to the notion of Julietta?"

"My dear sister-in-law thinks I should not be, and is devilishly persistent in her praises of her latest protegée. You would have thought, with her scarce concealed dislike of me, and resentment over my inheritance, that she would not be so urgent in her desire to see me leg-shackled," he continued musingly, refilling the empty glasses and carrying his own across to where, despite the warm evening, a fire glowed in the grate.

George considered his friend dispassionately. He frequently wondered why the Earl had for so long resisted the charms of the many beauties who had placed themselves or been thrust in his way since he had appeared in town. The determination of fond mamas to ensnare him had been increased since he had inherited his brother's title almost two years earlier.

Dermot, Earl of Heronforth, was a sight to set maiden hearts palpitating. Tall and slim, he was yet broad enough that his coats needed no padding at the shoulders, and muscular enough to show a fine leg. His face was not precisely handsome, for his features were not entirely regular, and his eyes, large and fine though they were, too often held an abstracted expression as he stared unseeingly at those who attempted to engage him in trivial conversation. But the women either did not notice, or were intrigued at his apparent aloofness. Since, apart from this, his manner was invariably polite and considerate to them, it did not seem to be of great moment that he rarely appeared to hear what they said.

"How much is that I owe you?" he asked now, his deep, pleasant voice breaking in on George's reflections. George consulted a paper beside him and added a figure.

"Three hundred," he said briefly.

"Shall we play again?"

"Indeed, and then let us dine. Do you propose going to the ball Lady Carruthers holds tonight?"

"I had thought to look in, if no more congenial entertainment offered," the Earl replied, returning to the table and cutting the cards.

For half an hour there was comparative silence as they concentrated on the game, and then a second time the Earl threw down his cards in disgust.

"You have me again."

"You are not up to form tonight," George answered lightly.

"I never was as good as James."

The Earl crossed to a small walnut bureau and unlocked it, taking out a rouleau of gold. He counted out the coins.

"Was James good?" George asked in

surprise. "I was much younger than he, of course, but I never saw him play."

"He did not from about the time he married Sylvia. I collect she complained, though as I was in the Peninsula at the time I did not know much about it. Before that he played an excessive amount and was very skilled."

"Why in the world did James marry Sylvia? It has always puzzled me, for she does not in the least seem the type of female to attract a Heronforth."

"James never did have much luck with his women, poor fellow," the Earl said, relocking the bureau.

"Then it was not perhaps so great a misfortune that he died at Waterloo. Though Sylvia would not think so!"

"Poor Sylvia. Her only child a girl, unable to inherit the title, and left with an adequate but not overgenerous jointure. Naturally she resents me!"

"If only she would not display it to all and sundry. It does her no good to be continually complaining."

"It does me no harm. But you have reminded me that she comes up to town in a few days."

"Is she still using the town house?"

"Oh yes, she prefers Berkeley Square, and it suits me to have the house opened for her. It would never otherwise be used, since I prefer to stay here in my rooms."

"That I can understand, for it is a gloomy barracks of a place. But she will have to make other arrangements when you marry."

The Earl laughed. "You do persist in this notion, George! Are you more foxed than I thought? I have no intention of being hustled into matrimony by the wishes, ill wishes, I might add, of my so-called friends!"

George grinned. "Then have a care, for the fair Julietta means to ensnare you if she and her mama and Sylvia can contrive it!"

"I shall have more to concern me these next few months," the Earl said with a slight grimace. "Your talk of James has reminded me."

George raised his eyebrows. "What in the world do you mean?"

"It is a long story."

"Then start it soon," he recommended,

helping himself to more wine.

The Earl sipped his own wine, gazing into the flames. Then he began, in a slightly mocking voice.

"I received a letter yesterday from the son of an old friend of James. He is coming to London and I have agreed to introduce him to the *ton.*"

"You have what?" George stared at his friend in fascinated disbelief. " It is you that are foxed, Dermot! Who the devil is this friend?"

The Earl grinned amiably at him. "I am not cast away, George, have no fear of that. I have no desire to bear-lead this young sprig about the town, but James promised to do it just before he went off to the continent, before he died. As I inherited all else from him, this is a part of it."

"Rather you than me," George said unsympathetically. "Your friends will wonder what the devil possesses you, trailing a stripling about. How old is the lad?"

"Just seventeen, I understand. But I hope that Sylvia will take him about with her. I have no desire to be accused of introducing an innocent into evil ways!"

George laughed. "Why did James agree? Has the lad no relatives of his own?"

"Apparently not. I did not know Robert Blain, James' friend, but I heard a great deal about him from James, and since James owes him so much I must take on the responsibility." He lapsed into silence for a while, gazing musingly into the flames. "It was like this," he went on slowly, "Robert Blain was a year or so older than James, and when James went to Eton he protected him from bullying. James had much illness as a child, and was not strong even then. Later, when they were both at Oxford, James became entangled with some harpy who would have tricked him into marriage if it had not been for Robert. He contrived in some manner to send her off. I never heard the full account, but I told you that James was a fool where women were concerned."

"Blain? I have heard the name, I think, but cannot recall having met this man. Odd his name is never mentioned."

"He had dropped out of society a great deal after his marriage, and almost completely these last six or seven years.

While protecting James from an early marriage, Robert fell into one himself. I do not say he was trapped, I think it was a most respectable, dull affair, but he was only just of age. Having escaped himself, I can remember James declaring that early marriages were the devil, and indeed he did not eventually marry until he was almost thirty."

"Having learned wisdom?" George queried, amused.

"Perhaps not," the Earl agreed. "After Robert married he spent most of his time on his estates in Dorset, enlarging his already vast fortune, and rarely came to town. He fathered this brat and when his wife died some years later, was saddled with him. That was about the time of James' marriage, and I do not think they saw each other after that."

"Was Sylvia jealous?"

"I do not think so. There was no cause, for after his marriage Robert had been immersed in his estates. He occasionally came up to town on business, but never spent the season here, possibly because his wife was in poor health. I do not know. It is likely that he disapproved of James' marriage. I doubt if he would consider Sylvia much better than the harpy at Oxford!"

"So the fortune hunting mamas will be after this youth. I do not envy you your task."

"The money is tied up with trustees until the lad is of age. I shall no doubt have to go and see them too," he said in disgust.

George laughed unsympathetically. "It will give you something to do, Dermot, to prevent you from becoming too bored!"

The Earl flashed him a quick glance. "Bored? With the follies of fashionable London to observe? And friends like you? Never!"

"And attacks by footpads to repel?" George interposed, referring to a recent episode when the footpads had received decidedly the worst of the encounter. "And women like Julietta to pursue or evade as your fancy dictates," he continued.

"As you say! Well, do we go to the ball?"

"Unless you prefer more cards?"

"I have had enough. My luck is out

tonight and I know when to declare a halt! You shall not pluck me any more tonight, George!"

"Then dinner. Where shall it be?"

"Dine here, and then we can go straight round to Lady Carruthers'."

George grimaced. "I am not overfond of Fielden's cooking. Why do you keep him?"

"He is an incomparable valet, and no-one puts a better shine on hessians. But you need not fear his cooking tonight. His niece has just arrived in London and stays with him until she can obtain a situation. She is an excellent cook, and I am thinking of retaining her. Can I tempt you?"

"In that case, yes, and you can tell me more of Robert Blain. I am still curious."

The Earl smiled, and rose to ring the bell. His valet appeared almost at once. Fielden was a slightly built man with quick darting eyes and sandy hair, and an air of contempt for all except his master, who was always obeyed with prompt efficiency.

"Can Betty provide us with dinner?"

"Indeed, yes, my lord, she has it all prepared, having said to me that you would be sure to invite your friend. There's a pair of spring chickens done to a turn, as well as pork cutlets, and some Rober sauce to go with them. And a veal pie, and some lobster soup, and a couple of tarts as well."

"Then we will sample them," the Earl said, breaking into this enthusiastic recital of the treats in store.

Turning to George as his man left the room he raised his eyebrows quizzically. "Will that be to your taste, George? It's clear Fielden thinks highly of his niece's abilities in the kitchen."

They preserved a companionable silence while Fielden came in with a loaded tray and swiftly laid the small table which he drew nearer to the fire. He bustled about fussily, then with as much pride as though he bore the dishes for a banquet, he carried in the culinary delights he had ennumerated to his master.

They set to, and George was pleasantly surprised at the quality of the meal.

"Far superior to Fielden's own efforts," he praised. "Hire the wench at once,

Dermot, and I shall dine here regularly!"

"I think I might, though as I shall be living in Berkeley Square for the next few months, it seems unnecessary."

"You can hardly introduce her there, Monsieur Henri would have hysterics!" George laughed, referring to the Earl's temperamental French chef. "But you are bound to want to come here on occasions for a bachelor party. Even though the house is yours you will not wish to spend all your time in Sylvia's company."

"True," the Earl agreed. "I might need to escape. That was what you had in mind?"

"From your protegé too."

"Young Bobby."

"Is that his name?" George asked, revolted.

The Earl laughed at his tone. "That was what Robert called him in the letter he wrote to James."

"Tell me more about the lad. Or do you know much?"

"Almost nothing. James received this letter two years ago, as I said, just before he went off to Brussels. It seems that Robert Blain was dying. I do not know

13

the details, except that he said he had only a few months to live, and asked James and Sylvia to take on the task of showing Bobby the town when he was seventeen. There is apparently an aunt, the sister of his wife, who was in charge in Dorset, and the lad was being educated at home."

"Why did he not send him to Eton?"

"I do not know. I could wish that he had, for a country bred lad, brought up by a no doubt doting spinster aunt, will be the very devil! I anticipate having to restrain him from all manner of mischief. Or he might be a lumpish yokel, and need to be pushed every step of the way, open-mouthed in astonishment at the wonders he observes!"

"Neither will suit Julietta. Whatever he is like, he will get in her way."

"That might be the only virtue to emerge from the whole scheme," the Earl said, grinning at him.

"Is Sylvia pleased at the idea?"

"I fancy not, though she talks a great deal about her duty to do all that James would have wished, and proses on about my responsibilities that I have inherited along with the position. She prates about duty until I am sickened of the word."

"And yet that is why you do it," his friend said percipiently, in a quiet tone.

"For James only," Heronforth returned shortly, and led the conversation onto other topics, asking which of their friends and acquaintances had arrived in town as yet, for the season was barely started. Fielden removed the covers and set a decanter of fine brandy between them, then quietly withdrew. The Earl poured out the brandy and sipped it appreciatively.

"I really do not care for parading at Lady Carruthers' ball, making insipid conversation with insipid damsels whose mamas hope that being on the scene thus early, they will catch the poor worms there," he said suddenly.

"You are hipped. Is it the wretched Bobby, or the fair Julietta?" George enquired.

"Both," responded the Earl, rising and prowling restlessly about the room.

"Sylvia seems more determined this time than ever before."

"She positively thrusts the girl under

my notice. She was greatly offended when I did not offer for Julietta last season. I had to evade a house party she organised a month ago, on some excuse. I fear that she encourages Julietta to hope too much. Yet I suppose I must marry some time and provide an heir, especially now I have the title. I confess I would be averse to thinking it would pass to Fitzjohn."

"Indeed no!" George shuddered. "Not that prosy old fool. But as you can give him more than fifteen years there seems little hope for him. Incidentally, I heard that he is selling up? Is that true?"

"It may be. He has been very short of the ready these last two years."

"And might be hoping for your early demise. You must disappoint him by marriage. But surely it does not have to be Julietta?"

"What have you against her? She is lovely, and amiable."

"Oh, she is a veritable beauty, I grant you. But she seems too concerned with pleasing you, and shows no will of her own."

"Admirable qualities in a wife, I should

have thought," the Earl commented, amused, leaning back against the mantle-piece.

George shook his head decisively.

"For some men, aye, but not for you, Dermot! Why, you would be confoundedly bored in less than a month."

Heronforth glanced at him. "Then recommend me a female that would not bore me," he suggested, half seriously. "I cannot, off hand, call one to mind."

"Neither can I," George said with a laugh. "Such a paragon does not exist."

"Save me from a paragon of virtue, at all events," the Earl shuddered. "It seems I am doomed."

"You will have to be content with the company of the stripling Bobby. When does he arrive?"

"In ten days. I have the letter here." He strolled across to a small table on which writing materials were spread, and picked up a sheet of paper. "Read it. What do you make of the lad?"

George perused the letter with some effort.

"Atrocious writing!" he commented. "They would not have permitted this at

Eton! Terse and to the point. A surly lad, possibly? He does not seem overanxious to come."

"Sylvia must deal with him, and the sooner he decides to retreat to Dorset the better pleased I shall be."

They sat for a moment, then George attempted to distract his friend by enquiring where they should spend the evening.

"Do you fancy Watier's?"

The Earl shook his head. "I have had my fill of gaming for today."

"Vauxhall then, let us see whom we can find there."

The Earl agreed, but made no move to straighten his cravat, or put to rights his disordered hair. In the silence the sounds of the street outside drifted to the two men. It was the hour when the members of the *ton* were setting off for fashionable parties or their clubs, and several carriages could be heard, with the occasional shout of a coachman as someone obstructed his way.

George eyed the Earl worriedly. Though he was often silent, and derived great amusement from observing the follies of his friends, he was rarely moody as he had been tonight. George wondered whether it was the prospect of accepting, out of apathy, a marriage with Julietta, or that of bear-leading the young Bobby Blain that cast him down so much. But he was not allowed much time to pursue these thoughts.

There arose a murmur of voices outside the room, and Fielden's was heard, raised in accents of protest. A high, feminine voice cut across his, but no words were distinguishable. The Earl glanced in annoyance at the door, and took a step towards it.

"What the devil goes on? If that is Betty making a commotion, I shall send her off instantly!"

The door opened and Fielden, his expression a comical mixture of apology and disgust, appeared. He seemed incapable of speech.

Heronforth raised his eyebrows. "Well, have you an explanation for that hubbub?" he asked coldly.

"I beg pardon, my lord, I'm sure. I would not have disturbed you, knowing that you do not wish to be disturbed, and thinking that you would not wish to be troubled by the young person — "

The Earl's expression had softened to one of amusement. "What is amiss, Fielden?" he asked calmly, but the man was not to be hurried.

"I told the young person that you would not wish to be disturbed, so late in the day as it is, and that if she returned tomorrow at a respectable hour, you would no doubt condescend to see her," he continued, unperturbed. "But she would not be denied, and has some faradiddle that you are expecting her," he concluded, the repugnance in his tone indicating clearly what he thought of such an unlikely tale.

"And so he is, you great looby. If you could bring yourself to stop talking fustian, and announce me, the Earl would be a great deal wiser," a girl's voice, high and clear, came from behind him.

Fielden swung round, his mouth open to administer some reproof, but the visitor, taking advantage of the gap thus left in the doorway, slipped quickly through it followed by her companion. She stood there, her head tilted slightly to one side, composedly surveying the room and its occupants.

"Which of you is the Earl of Heronforth?" she asked after a moment of stunned silence, glancing from one to the other, a gleam of amusement in her eyes as she took in their disorder and noted the wine glasses on the table.

They stared back speechless for a moment. She was tall, slenderly built but shapely, as her tightly fitting pelisse clearly demonstrated. Her face was heart shaped, and her eyes, a vivid blue, seemed enormous as she stared at them. Beneath a fetching bonnet they could see that she possessed an unruly mass of short, red-gold curls. A smile curved her lips, and an enchanting dimple appeared.

The Earl recovered his wits, and while one hand strayed unconsciously to his hopelessly disordered cravat, the other waved to Fielden to go.

"I will ring when I need you," he said abruptly, then turned to the girl, noticing briefly that a pale, frightened looking woman in her early thirties stood beside her.

"I have not the pleasure of your

acquaintance, I collect?" he said smoothly, bowing to them both. "I am Heronforth. Pray will you be seated, and tell me to what I owe this visit?"

The girl looked at him as she and her companion took the chairs George hastened to pull out for them, and a slight frown creased her brow.

"But are you not expecting us? I own, I was puzzled after having received your invitation to find that the house in Berkeley Square was closed, and to be directed here by the porter, but surely you have had my letter telling you of our arrival?"

"I am at a loss, I must confess. May I introduce my friend, Mr George Fenton? You are — ?"

He paused, raising his eyebrows at her and smiling encouragingly, and she acknowledged George's greeting abstractedly.

"How do you do, Mr Fenton? My lord, it was arranged that you would receive me, or rather that your wife would, long ago. I sent you one letter and received a reply that you would be expecting me, and a week since I sent to notify you of the date we would arrive."

"But who are you?" the Earl demanded, wanting confirmation of the suspicions that had occurred to him.

"Roberta Blain. My father was a great friend of yours, long ago — although you do not look nearly so old as he did," she added consideringly, causing George to turn away and bury his face in a handkerchief hurriedly dragged out of his pocket, into which he sneezed unconvincingly.

"Bobby!" the girl's companion protested, and with a start the Earl recollected her presence and turned towards her.

"I do beg your pardon! My wits have gone a-begging. Miss Blain, will you not introduce me?"

The girl smiled. "My dear Aunt Rose, Miss Holt, who has cared for me since my mama died."

"Welcome, Miss Holt. I am exceedingly sorry to appear so unprepared. Will you and your niece take some refreshment? Have you dined?"

"We have dined, my lord, but some wine would be very welcome," Miss Blain replied, her aunt appearing lost for words.

The Earl turned towards the table, but was forestalled by George who poured out the wine which he carried across to the ladies. He then stationed himself to the side from where he had an uninterrupted view of Miss Blain's delightful profile.

"Were you not expecting me, my lord?" she asked, after a slight pause, during which the Earl stared at her, bemused.

He grinned engagingly.

"Not precisely. You see, I read your letter for the thirtieth, not the twentieth, and — it's a little difficult, for I was under the impression that your father's child was a son."

He was watching Miss Blain's face, and admiring the even white teeth that showed between her full lips as she suddenly laughed, realising how the confusion had arisen, and it was George who, with an exclamation, sprang forward to catch Miss Holt as she moaned and subsided in a swoon towards the floor.

2

BOBBY and the young man accompanying her rode in silence across the open hillside, from where they could, on clear days, see the waves pounding onto the long sandy shore that curved gently round the wide bay. Bobby had plenty of plans to occupy her thoughts, and was oblivious of the anxious glances cast at her every few yards by her companion.

He was a few years older than she, large and muscular but already inclining to fat, as his incipient double chin demonstrated. His lank, light brown hair flopped untidily, and he continually pushed it away from his eyes.

At last he spoke, hoarsely. "Bobby." Not hearing him, absorbed as she was in her own thoughts, Bobby rode on and he had to repeat her name loudly before she turned to look enquiringly at him out of her cool blue eyes that so often, he thought with one of his rare flashes of imagination, looked like the blocks of ice stored deep underground on his father's land, for use in the summer to keep the food fresh.

"What is it, Edward?"

She spoke in a friendly enough manner, but he seemed to have difficulty in proceeding.

"Well?" she added, a trace of the impatience that often assailed her when she was dealing with Edward creeping into her voice.

He gulped, and pushed the errant lock of hair aside.

"My mother," he at last ejaculated.

"What about her? I wish you would overcome this habit of speaking in monosyllables," she chided, irritated.

"I know. I know you don't like it. I'm sorry, I'll try."

She restrained herself from comment, hoping that he would at last say what it was he wanted. He often lapsed into this condition of incoherence when it was something momentous that concerned him. If he were extolling the virtues of his horses or dogs, or describing the last hunting expedition, he could wax lyrical in comparison with his drawing room conversation. He gulped again, several times, and unconsciously halted his horse. Some paces ahead of him Bobby also reined in and turned round to survey him.

"Will you do as she says?" he asked eventually, his urgency causing him to slur the words together so that Bobby had difficulty in making out their meaning. She understood enough to avoid having to ask for a repetition.

"What your mother says? What do you mean? She has said rather a lot of things today," she added ruefully, recalling the constant stream of chatter, mostly inane, that had assailed her ears during her visit to Lady Staple.

"About London," he stammered.

Light dawned, and Bobby grinned understandingly at him. "I see. When she pressed me to spend part of the season with her in Mount Street?"

He nodded, pleased that she had understood his meaning so swiftly.

"You won't, will you?" he asked wistfully, and she laughed.

"How very ungallant you sound," she mocked.

He looked puzzled, and then, realising what he had said, blushed a fiery red.

"I did not — she — you know — "

Miserably he faltered into silence and stared helplessly at her.

"I'm teasing, Edward, for I collect you do not mean to be impolite. I have no desire to sound ungrateful to your mama, but you must know how exceedingly difficult it would be for me to spend a great deal of time in her company. We have so little in common. She has been kind to me, inviting me over so frequently since Papa died — "

"Not kind. Wants me to marry you. For your fortune," he put in, succinctly but with absolute clarity of meaning.

Bobby grinned. "I know. And you do not wish that in the least, do you, Edward?"

"She says I must make an offer for you," he said reluctantly.

"And that is why she wants us to be in London together. When I said that I was intending to pass the season there, she suggested, most generously, that I went as her guest. You need have no fear, Edward, I will not!"

He smiled, relieved, and set his horse in motion again.

"She will be in a miff." He spoke more easily now that his main worry was disposed of, and with a certain relish.

"I hope she will not place the blame on you."

He shrugged. "She always does. It makes no difference. Father and I keep out of her way as much as possible."

Bobby nodded, certain that she would do precisely that if it were her fate to have to live in close proximity to Lady Staple. Sir John was a hearty, bluff man, with a friendly word for all his tenants, and on good terms with all his neighbours. His wife was altogether different, a scheming, far from intelligent woman, who doted on her only son and tried to force him into paths he was totally unfitted to follow. Her latest scheme, conceived when Bobby's father had died two years earlier, had been to marry Edward to the heiress. She had contrived to throw them together as much as possible, and had endeavoured to instill into the reluctant Edward's head that he must offer for Bobby before she had an opportunity of meeting other, more attractive suitors. She did not deceive herself as to her son's shortcomings, and was well aware that Bobby, beautiful and vivacious as she was, would be sure to attract many offers once she came out into society.

Disappointed of her hopes so far by Edward's mulish refusal to overcome his shyness and speak to Bobby, she had been startled by Bobby's announcement that she intended to go to London that year, but had countered swiftly with an invitation to stay with them. It had been an uncharacteristically swift, as well as generous decision, for she had previously decided not to afford the expense of a London season that year. The prize was too alluring: the offer had been made, and even though Bobby had refused it in a most decided manner, she had on that instant determined to be on hand in London, able to fight for the preservation of her objective.

Bobby, secretly amused at this patently obvious manoeuvre, had politely evaded questions about her plans, saying that all was not yet decided, and no, she was not yet certain where she would be living, or with whom, or even when she would set out for the metropolis. Baulked, Lady Staple had drawn Edward aside and again urged on him the necessity of his speaking to the heiress soon, before the prize slipped from his grasp. Then, with a false smile for Bobby, she had sent them off on the ride to Bobby's home five miles away.

They had almost reached the house. It was of modest proportions, built of the local grey stone by Bobby's grandfather, and now surrounded by the trees he had planted, so that although it looked down the slopes of the gently rolling hills directly towards the sea, it was sheltered from the gales that sometimes swept up from the shore, even on this normally temperate coast.

They rode along the drive that wound, lined by a thick belt of trees, from the road that bordered the estate on the east. Before the house, which was built round a courtyard, was a wide terrace with a stable block to the side, hidden by more trees. They skirted the terrace and made for this. Bobby's groom, an elderly man who had held her on her first pony, and who was also her coachman on the few occasions when she used that mode of transport, came to meet her and took her horse as she sprang down. She turned to Edward, who had not been so quick and was still mounted.

"Thank you for your escort, Edward. No, pray do not dismount. You must hurry to reach home again before dark. Say all that is proper to your mama for me."

Edward stared down at her, suddenly dismayed at the prospect of returning home and confessing that he had, after the excellent opportunity of a long ride alone together, still not made an offer to Bobby.

"Mama, she said I was to ask you — " he pleaded, fluent in his desperation.

Bobby cut in ruthlessly. "Tell her you attempted it, and I would not listen," she recommended blithely. He looked aghast, knowing this to be beyond his powers, and she grinned up at him. "It will be true. I am going in now. Do not look so shatter-brained, for she cannot compel you, after all."

Before he could answer, she had run

across to a side door that led into the kitchen quarters, turning briefly to wave before she disappeared.

"She's a right caution, our Miss Bobby!" Shearer, the groom, laughed throatily, and Edward looked at him uncomprehendingly. The man grinned, and led Bobby's horse away into his stall. Realising that he had been deserted, Edward turned his own mount and went slowly from the yard, unaware that Bobby was observing his reluctant departure from a window on the landing.

She breathed a sigh of relief, and dismissing him from her mind went to change into a fresh, sprigged muslin gown. She dragged a brush through her tangled curls, and bound them with a blue ribbon that matched the one on her gown.

Then she descended to the morning room which her Aunt Rose used as a sitting room in preference to the rather ornate double drawing room on the other side of the house.

"Hello, my dear, did you have a pleasant day?" Aunt Rose asked, setting aside her sewing and smiling fondly at her niece as

Bobby bent to kiss her.

Bobby grimaced. "With Lady Staple? Aunt, you cannot imagine for one moment that that would be possible?"

"Oh, I dare say it might. She is a good hearted woman, though somewhat of a ninny," Aunt Rose said consideringly.

"She is bird-witted," Bobby said bluntly, and Aunt Rose winced slightly, but did not reprove her niece, for secretly she approved of the stronger description.

"Did Edward escort you home?"

"Oh, yes, poor lad. I vow, the way his mother hag-rides him is abominable. That a grown man, and Edward is all of three and twenty, should permit it is past my understanding!"

"Yes, my dear, for it would never do for you," Aunt Rose replied with a smile. "But though she is unwise, I consider her to be well intentioned. And he is a dutiful son, to be sure."

"Too dutiful! But enough of the Staples, Aunt. I have been thinking more of the plan I discussed with you last night, and I am quite decided on it."

"Oh dear," Aunt Rose uttered despondently. "Do you think it would really be wise, my love?"

"I am determined, especially after today! I shall write this very night to the Earl of Heronforth, and remind him of the promise he gave Papa that his wife would bring me out when I was of age. He cannot object to that."

"It might be inconvenient," her aunt protested, but unconvincingly, for she knew that her objections would be swept aside by her strong-minded niece.

"If so, they will tell us, but until we write they cannot do so," Bobby argued reasonably. "If this year it is for any reason totally impossible for them, I must contrive otherwise, but you know that this is by far the most suitable scheme."

"If they could not receive you this year, you could wait, possibly, until next?" Aunt Rose asked, clutching at the faint hope of delaying, if not evading the issue.

"By next year I am like to be married to cousin Jeremy," Bobby said slowly.

"Then he could take you to London," Aunt Rose suggested, her hopes lifting.

"Jeremy never stirs from his estates for a moment longer than is absolutely essential," Bobby answered, dismissing this idea. "I should not be able to drag him to London for a whole season, and besides, I would most likely be doing my duty by him and breeding lots of little Holts to inherit our fortunes."

"Bobby!" Aunt Rose was truly scandalised at this. "Your conversation is, to say the least, indelicate, my child," she said reprovingly when she was able to trust herself to speak calmly. "It will not do in polite circles, I assure you!"

Bobby grinned at her, unrepentant. "I only say it to you, my love, not in company. But as it is natural and the truth, and Jeremy is always talking to me of his farm animals and their progeny, I do not see why I should be bashful."

"Perhaps not, but I really would prefer you not to say such things even to me."

"I will try to remember, dear Aunt Rose. But you do see why it is essential to make a push to go to London this year?"

"I hope it is not that you are averse to the notion of marrying your cousin?"

Aunt Rose said a trifle wistfully. "He is a fine upright man, who will not gamble away your dear father's fortune, and who will care for you in the way both your dear parents would have wished."

"Yes. I appreciate that he is your favourite nephew," Bobby rejoined, laughing at her, "and that his father was the very best of brothers! I am sure Jeremy is a paragon, but — do you not think he is — just a trifle — *dull*? He would never cause his wife the slightest anxiety!"

"You talk nonsense," Aunt Rose answered robustly. "No wife wants to be caused any anxiety, and no sensible girl would consider for a moment marrying a man that shows any disposition for wildness."

"It might be more fun," Bobby said irrepressibly, then hurried on before her aunt could read her a lecture. "At least Jeremy is far more admirable than Edward."

"Edward?" Aunt Rose was diverted. "You cannot mean that he has made you an offer?"

"Oh no, despite his mother's firm instructions!"

"That woman!"

"Yes, I agree. But not even the prospect of her anger would induce Edward to marry me. We are agreed on that."

"You have discussed it with him?" Aunt Rose said, scandalised afresh at her niece's unladylike behaviour.

"I had to put him out of his misery and tell him that it would not do, that I would never marry him whatever he said, and so he need not be put to the inconvenience of making me an offer. I did not say it precisely so, but I made him understand me."

"Bobby!" her aunt moaned. "What will you do next?"

"Go to London for the season."

"The Earl is most unlikely to be able to receive you."

"Well, I utterly refuse to go with Lady Staple, though she was most pressing with an invitation when I told her that I was going. That would be insupportable by any reckoning! But she was of the opinion, I collect, that it would aid Edward."

"The woman's a fool! It would be more likely to frighten you away if you did have a *tendre* towards him," Aunt Rose exclaimed.

"She would hardly see it in that light," Bobby said charitably. "What alternative is there? We could set up our own establishment, but we have no relatives or friends in London who could introduce us to the *ton*, and I am persuaded that two females in such a situation would not be regarded favourably. Particularly as we would have no male acquaintances."

"No, that would never do," Aunt Rose agreed fervently. "But we know nothing at all about the Earl of Heronforth. Living so retired as we do here in the country, we hear so little of London gossip, and I have never heard his name mentioned. How can we be certain that he and his wife are — well, suitable people to be in charge of you?"

Bobby gurgled in amusement. "Aunt Rose! You must not disparage a member of the aristocracy! That will not do at all!"

"A title does not confer good manners and impeccable behaviour," her aunt answered tartly. "You have only to look at the Prince Regent and his brothers to know that even the highest in the land can be disreputable!"

"I thought you did not care for me to gossip about the Royal Princes, Aunt?" Bobby said in dulcet tones, and Aunt Rose, realising that in her agitation she had let her tongue run away with her, blushed rosy red with mortification. Bobby laughed and went to put her arms about her aunt.

"I fear I have not brought you up as your dear mother would have wished," Aunt Rose sighed.

"Fustian! You cannot keep gossip about the Princes away from me, however quiet a life we lead. And as we have not heard any about the Earl, at least he does not appear to be one of their set. I suppose he is too young. Let me see, he was two years younger than Father, who would now be almost forty, so he is six or seven and thirty or thereabouts. And as he *was* a friend of Papa, there can be no question of his fitness."

"No, your Papa would undoubtedly not have been friends with a rake or a gambler," Aunt Rose admitted.

"And he asked for the Earl's promise

when he knew he was dying."

That was incontrovertible, and Aunt Rose did not attempt to produce any further objections.

"Then I suppose it must be as you wish," she capitulated.

Bobby kissed her.

"I should like to have one season's enjoyment in London, for I suppose I will eventually marry Jeremy and spend the rest of my life buried in Cornwall," she remarked a little wistfully, and her aunt was quite overcome at this. For the first time a doubt assailed her as to the wisdom of her hopes that her niece and nephew would be happy together. It had been suggested long ago. Bobby had grown up with the idea and had never objected,but now Aunt Rose wondered if Jeremy, staid and reliable, but possibly dull, was the right husband for the volatile, energetic Bobby. It was true that life with Jeremy would be rather tame, she admitted, but it would be safe. Better, she decided suddenly, to allow Bobby some freedom to indulge her high spirits now, before she married.

"Shall I write the letter to the Earl?" she

asked, burying her doubts and prepared to enter wholeheartedly into Bobby's plans.

"No. I will do it. I have taken you away from your mending for long enough, and we shall have lots of sewing to do to prepare us for London," Bobby answered gaily, and went to seat herself at the escritoire in the corner of the room.

"Be careful with your writing then," Aunt Rose warned.

Bobby grinned across at her, and busied herself with quill and paper. When the letter was finished Aunt Rose glanced through it, shaking her head at the bold, untidy writing, but aware that it would be no better done if she insisted on a fairer copy. Bobby sealed the missive with a wafer, wished her aunt goodnight and went to her room.

She was content at having persuaded her Aunt Rose to the plan. She had used many arguments but not the one that, to her, was the only important one. However, she knew that were her aunt to discover this objective of her visit to London she would never agree to accompany her. Even Bobby was unwilling to set out for London alone.

This urgent reason was to clear her father's name. Bobby had adored her handsome and clever father, and they had been very close after her mother died when she was ten. In the months before his death, when he had been confined to his bed, he had told her a good deal about his early life. Once he had rather bitterly told her that he had retired from society after her mother's death because on his last visit to London, six years ago, he had unjustly been accused of cheating at cards. To Bobby, aware that her father was the soul of honour, and known throughout the county as the fairest of landlords, the merest suggestion of dishonesty was horrifying. Grimly her father had replied to her protests that the slightest accusation might be sufficient to ruin a man, but he was unable to declare the truth and clear himself without involving many others, who would be made very unhappy if he did. For himself, he no longer cared, after his wife's recent death, having lost all desire for London society. He had not explained to her the details, but once, when he had been almost asleep, he had murmured that Fitzjohn knew the truth.

Bobby had no idea who this was, but had remembered the name and determined to seek out the man to discover from him the truth of the story. Then she could proclaim her father's innocence, feeling that this would be a gift to him in return for the exceedingly happy childhood he had given her.

She was sure that her aunt, despite her admiration for her dead sister's husband, would strongly object to her niece's involvement in anything so unsavoury, and meant to do all possible to protect her aunt from knowledge of it.

A few days later the Earl's reply was received, to say that it would be convenient to receive her and Miss Holt as proposed. There was no warmth in the letter, which was couched in the most formal of terms, and no reference to the Countess, which put Aunt Rose into a flutter.

"What of it?" Bobby demanded. "You surely cannot expect a long gossipy letter to someone who is not even an acquaintance yet? He is willing to take us, and that is all that matters."

Her aunt's qualms, however, temporarily

subdued on the night that Bobby had written the letter, and firmly suppressed later with the thought that it was a wild scheme unlikely to lead to anything, had been reawoken. She spent the days between the arrival of the Earl's missive and their departure for London in a state of dithering anxiety that nearly drove Bobby to distraction, and taxed her patience to the limit. But she had a very real affection for her aunt, and realised that the prospect of London was much more daunting for Aunt Rose than for herself. That lady had spent a most unhappy season there for her own coming out fifteen years or so earlier, and had afterwards retired thankfully to the peace and tranquility of the country. When Bobby's mother, after suffering two dangerous pregnancies in quick succession, and the loss of two children, had asked for help in her own weakened state of health, Rose had gladly accepted the invitation to live with her sister and had remained a part of the household ever since.

Bobby set about the preparations for the journey with her usual brisk efficiency.

She sent a note to the Earl telling him when to expect them, sent their heavy trunks ahead by carrier, and then, one fine spring morning, she and her aunt set out to post for London, both with rather mixed feelings now that the time had arrived.

3

BOBBY wasted no time in exclamations, but her lips twitched in amusement as George turned frantic eyes towards her, awkwardly clasping to him the limp form of Miss Holt. She rose from her chair and calmly dashed the wine from her almost full glass ruthlessly into her aunt's face. Heronforth blinked at the coolness of the action and the use to which his excellent wine was put, but he had to admit it was an effective remedy, for Miss Holt began to moan faintly.

"Lay her down on the sofa, if you will be so kind," Bobby directed George and he, bemused, but thankful to be relieved of his embarrassing encumbrance, did so with some alacrity. Bobby had retrieved the reticule her aunt had let fall, and pulled from it a small bottle.

"Hold these smelling salts under her nose," she commanded, thrusting the bottle into the Earl's hand, and went to loosen her aunt's pelisse, unbuttoning it at the neck and then settling her comfortably with her head on a cushion.

"She will soon be recovered, my lord," she said encouragingly to the Earl, who was kneeling beside the sofa meekly obeying her instructions.

George choked, and tried to turn it into a cough, and then blushed to find Bobby's frank gaze, her eyes alight with amusement, fixed on him for a moment before she turned back to minister to her aunt.

"She has these turns quite frequently," she said calmly, gently chafing her aunt's hands. "Come now, Aunt Rose, you will soon be feeling quite the thing. Do you care for a drink? Mr Fenton, some wine, if you would be so good! No, Aunt Rose, lie still! You shall sit up when you are completely better."

As the stricken lady appeared to be reviving under her expert administrations, the Earl thankfully rose and retreated across the room, resolutely refusing to meet George's eye.

Gradually Aunt Rose's senses returned, and she recalled the conversation. She insisted on sitting up and Bobby, seeing that there was more colour in her cheeks, did not demur. Miss Holt looked round at the two men, and attempted a pathetic smile.

"I do beg your pardon, my lord, for behaving in so — so *very* tiresome a way. But it was a great shock, you see. How could you possibly think Bobby was a boy?"

Exhibiting an admirable degree of self possession, the Earl refrained from glancing at George, who seemed to be having more trouble with his vocal chords, and smiled kindly at the distressed woman.

"Do not put yourself about, Miss Holt. I have only ever seen your niece's name, and in the letter she wrote me, there was no hint that she was a female. I assumed Bobby to be the name of a boy."

"But surely, as you were a friend of my father, you must have known!" Bobby exclaimed in disbelief.

Heronforth shook his head. "I fear there is another misapprehension. It was my older brother James who was your father's friend, not I. I inherited the title when James died two years ago, at

Waterloo, soon after your father's death, I believe. You cannot have heard that."

"Then — then why did you say that you would receive me and introduce me to the *ton*?" Bobby asked bluntly.

"My brother had promised, and I keep his promises for him."

"But you were not, I believe, ready to receive us in Berkeley Square?" Miss Holt intervened. "There must be some mistake. We should not have come," she wailed, her voice rising as she turned to Bobby.

"Hush, Aunt Rose, and let us disentangle this puzzle. I wrote again to you, my lord, after you replied that you would be ready to welcome us, giving you the date of our arrival."

The Earl had been looking at the letter he had earlier shown to George.

"I can see now what must have happened. I read the date of your arrival as the thirtieth, and the figure is a two, not a three. That is how the misunderstanding arose."

"Oh, Bobby, your dreadful writing! I knew that it would get you into a scrape one day," her aunt cried. "We must go to an hotel, my lord. Can you please direct us to a quiet, respectable one?"

"No, that is not to be thought on. I regret that my house in Berkeley Square is not open. It was to have been when Sylvia came up from the country, so I can arrange tomorrow for it to be ready. It is too late for you to go to an hotel tonight. You must stay here. My man's niece will look after you, and I will go with George to his rooms."

"Of course, Dermot, most welcome," George put in hastily, taking his eyes away for a moment from Miss Blain's enchanting countenance. As he looked back at her he was rewarded by a brilliant smile.

Miss Holt began to protest, but Bobby cut in decidedly.

"That is an excellent notion, and we shall be most comfortable here. Thank you, my lord, I am most grateful."

"No, Bobby, my love, we cannot possibly put the Earl to so much trouble," Miss Holt managed.

"You are unfit to go further," Bobby stated. "You know that after one of your turns you need a good sleep, and I think it very bad in you to refuse the Earl's most generous offer."

She subsided, too overwhelmed to argue, and sat mutely while the Earl disappeared to give instructions to his servants, and George made polite enquiries about their journey. But by the time the Earl returned, she had thought of another cause for concern.

"Your wife, my lord? You said that she was coming up from the country. Will it not be inconvenient for her to find us already installed in her house?"

"My wife! I am not married ma'am! Oh, lord, I see how this further misapprehension has occurred. Sylvia is my late brother's wife, and she was to be my hostess for the season, and take your — niece about. She has no town house of her own, and always uses mine. Naturally, now that you are here, and the mistake has been discovered, she will be much more involved in presenting Miss Blain."

"Will she be very pleased at that, if she was expecting a young man?" Bobby asked, gazing at him steadily.

He smiled. "Naturally she will be surprised, and Sylvia will need to adjust to the idea. It always takes time for her to do that, but I hope that you will be good for her, Miss Blain. My sister-in-law has had much to bear, losing her husband so soon, and with only one child, a daughter, to console her. Your company will distract her, and so you will be doing me more of a favour than I expected when I answered your letter. And now, I am sure Miss Holt will wish to retire, so if you will excuse me while I collect a few necessities, George and I will take ourselves off and leave you in peace. I will see you in the morning."

Within minutes he and Mr Fenton had departed, and Betty, round eyed at this sudden advent of two ladies whose comfort was to be her responsibility, brought them a tray of tea and biscuits, and informed them that their rooms would soon be ready.

"I've put you, Miss Holt, in the Earl's room, and Miss Blain in the small guest chamber, and I do hope as how you'll both be comfortable. I'm heating bricks now for the beds."

"Thank you, Betty, I'm persuaded you will look after us admirably," Bobby said briskly, and nodded dismissal.

"Bobby, this is deplorable! We must return home tomorrow!" Aunt Rose began as soon as the door was closed.

"Why so?" Bobby asked, genuinely surprised.

"We *cannot* stay with an unmarried man!" her aunt replied in horrified accents.

"We are not. We shall be staying with his widowed sister-in-law, as I understand it," Bobby said bracingly.

"But, but, he is not your father's friend!"

"But Sylvia was his wife, and she would have had most to do with me in any event. Aunt, now I am here I do not intend to give up my plans!"

"No, I had not thought you would," her aunt replied dolefully, and made intermittent lamentations until she was tucked up in the Earl's large, comfortable bed, and Bobby was able to kiss her goodnight and escape to her own reflections about this development in her plans.

George Fenton's rooms were just around the corner, but by the time they had walked there the Earl was already a little disturbed by the uninterrupted flow of praise for his protegée that poured from his friend.

"One would think you had never seen a pretty girl before," he said sharply when he was able to intervene.

"Pretty? She's beautiful! Incomparable! She'll take the town by storm. Those roguish eyes! Sylvia will be besieged by would-be suitors begging for an introduction!"

"Then you had best establish your interest before they discover her," his friend advised, a trifle sourly.

"Me?" George was silent for a moment, and then laughed uncertainly. " You know, I had thought I was not a marrying man, but I'll be damned if I'm not changing my mind!"

The Earl laughed suddenly. "She'll lead any man a dance! I would advise caution, George, before taking her on! She's wild, you can see from her eyes. And unbroken, a real handful!"

"Armful, rather," George replied with a laugh. "I wonder what Julietta will make of her?"

"Julietta?" The Earl seemed startled.

"It will be interesting to see," he said after a slight pause. "I'd best send Sylvia the news and prepare her. She is due in town in two days, but I do not suppose even this will induce her to come earlier. But I shall be spared the necessity of bear-leading! Perhaps it is all for the best, despite the inconvenience to you of having me sleep on your sofa!"

"For the opportunity of a close acquaintance with the delectable Bobby even that can be borne," George replied swiftly.

The Earl slept badly, an uncommon occurrence with him, and it was not entirely due to the sofa he slept on. He was awake far too early, in his friend's opinion, and demanding coffee from George's man while George himself sprawled beside the table watching Heronforth prowl restlessly about the room.

"You cannot call on them at this hour," George remarked disgustedly as Heronforth poured himself a cup of the steaming coffee and took it across to the window, where he stood sipping it and gazing down into the street.

"I must order things at Heronforth House," the Earl replied, smiling. "I have no desire to thrust my company on the ladies, but I will confess that the sooner I have them installed in Berkeley Square and can return to my rooms the better pleased I will be, for your sofa is confoundedly uncomfortable!"

"Then if you will be occupied, I will call on the ladies, at a seasonable hour, and offer my services. There may be — er — things, they require."

"Which Fielden and Betty cannot procure for them, I suppose?" the Earl asked coolly.

"The devil! They need some advice, for they must be feeling confused," George said hopefully.

"Miss Holt is like to be, but not Miss Bobby Blain, unless I am much mistook. She is undoubtedly revelling in the situation!"

Bobby was not precisely revelling in it, though she had derived considerable amusement since their arrival, in between soothing her aunt's bouts of dismay and self recriminations about their criminal carelessness in not having discovered that there was a new Earl, from recalling the shocked looks and the helplessness on the faces of the two men the previous evening. In fact the Earl's face had kept reappearing in her mind after she had retired to bed, and she had slept ill, disturbed by the gleam of amusement she kept recalling in his large, dark eyes. The way his lips curved was most attractive, she had thought, then hastily reminded herself that as she had met so few personable men in Dorset, she was really not qualified to judge. At one stage, half asleep, she had caught herself imagining that she was stroking back that disordered hair, so dark, and with, she was sure, a vital springiness. Blushing hotly at her own disordered thoughts, she had firmly turned her mind on what she needed in order to replenish her wardrobe, drifting off to sleep finally without realising that she had been mentally surveying the furnishings of the Earl's rooms in an attempt to guess which were his favourite colours.

Despite her restless night, Bobby, used to country hours, was up early, and was soon impatiently ringing the bell to ask

Fielden when she might expect the Earl to call.

"Why, it's barely nine o'clock!" that servitor exclaimed, horror struck. "The Earl would not dream of calling on a lady before noon!"

"Noon! Then what in the world am I to occupy myself with until then?"

Fielden did not deign to offer any suggestions, staring woodenly at a point over Bobby's left shoulder. She was amused, but almost immediately her thoughts had darted in another direction.

"Can you tell me where I might be able to engage a maid?"

Fielden's eyes flickered, and for a wild moment he wondered if this might be an opportunity for him to advance his niece, but just as he was reluctantly confessing to himself that Betty's talents lay more in the kitchen than in waiting upon a fashionable young lady, Bobby put paid to the idea entirely.

"I want a French maid, if at all possible, the best. One that can sew finely and is proficient at dressing hair. Can you tell me which are the best agencies?"

"I will go myself and explain your

requirements," he volunteered, unbending to her in response to this evidence of common sense that she showed in asking for his advice.

"If they have any suitable ones I would wish to see them here today," Bobby said, seeing with some amusement this activity also being taken from her.

"You cannot ask for them to come here!" Fielden exclaimed in tones of dismay, shaken from his habitual calm.

"Why ever not? Oh, you think the Earl would not care for it? Perhaps not."

"No respectable young lady would come!" Fielden stated firmly. "It is well known as the Earl's address, and you would be doing him a great disservice to advertise that a French maid is required here!"

Bobby suppressed a giggle. "Am I not respectable then?" she asked sweetly.

"It is a different matter," he replied, looking offended.

"Then I suppose I may interview them at Heronforth House when we remove there? When is that likely to be?"

"Today, my master said. I know that all is in readiness for her ladyship to arrive tomorrow, but he intends to install you and Miss Holt there today in the care of his housekeeper, Mrs Chase. Will there be anything else Miss?"

"No, thank you Fielden."

Bobby allowed him to escape, and amused herself with inspecting the Earl's sitting room, which was tastefully and comfortably furnished, containing many prints and books that bore witness to his sporting interests. Eventually she sat down at the table with two packs of cards and laid out a game of Demon Patience. This occupied her attention for a while, but when the game was blocked she swept the cards together with an exclamation of disgust. A low chuckle came from behind her, and she swung round to see the Earl standing just inside the door and surveying her in some amusement.

"So you do not cheat," he commented.

She was taken aback. "Of course not! It would be silly in patience for I would know it and the game would not have been truly won. I had not realised you were there."

"No, and I must crave pardon for intruding on you. The fact is, I am so accustomed to walking straight in that I failed to recall that today the room is yours."

"And you will be delighted to be rid of us," she laughed. "It was excessively kind in you to take pity on Aunt Rose last night, and I am truly grateful. She could have gone no further. Fielden says we may remove to Heronforth House today. That is, and I must ask you now that you have had time to consider it, if you are still prepared to receive me?"

"But naturally," he replied.

"You do not have to be polite. The situation is not as you expected. If it is distasteful for you I quite understand. I would ask just the favour that you assist me in finding a small house or lodging where we may stay, and possibly give me a few introductions to establish us creditably with the *ton*."

"I am not being merely polite," he assured her. "My sister-in-law, Sylvia, will benefit from your company. As for me, I have cause to be grateful to your father for his care of James, and this is my repayment. I will not permit you to take your aunt away."

"Well, if you are really certain." She smiled enchantingly at him, and he sat down opposite her, idly shuffling the cards.

"When your aunt is ready, Betty will prepare us a nuncheon, and I will escort you to Heronforth House and introduce you to Mrs Chase."

"That is kind. I have already asked Fielden for assistance in hiring a maid. My own is so countrified that I dared not bring her to London. I trust you would not object if I interviewed the girls at Heronforth House? Fielden was quite put out when I suggested doing so here!"

She eyed him mischievously, and he shot a startled glance at her.

"I had not realised that such a construction might be put upon the fact that a French maid was to be interviewed at the Earl of Heronforth's rooms. It seems that *no-one* is safe from gossip!" she concluded demurely, and he chuckled.

"It is insupportable to have one's actions so misconstrued," he rejoined, shaking his head dolorously, and Bobby giggled. "Of course you may," he went on, "but will not your aunt attend to that for you?"

"Aunt Rose? No. She is a dear, but would not have the least notion of how to deal with these girls, or know what I require. She would most like engage the first one, not liking to reject her. I am used to contriving a great deal myself, you must know."

"I can see that you are most capable," he replied, amused. "Not a managing female, I trust," he said softly, but she merely grinned at him and did not rise to the lure. "Pray treat Heronforth House as your own, and if I can be of any assistance to you, do not hesitate to call on me."

"I will remember, and I thank you. Now perhaps I had best see if my aunt is awake."

She left him, and he sat considering whether this second meeting had confirmed his impressions. She was a most determined female, and fully capable of getting her own way, he mused, without employing the wiles that any other girl with her astounding beauty would have used as second nature. He wondered what she and Sylvia would make of each other. Unbidden, the contrast between Bobby and Julietta came into his mind, and he smiled at the thought of Julietta's submissive ways, her anxiety to please, and the pretty way she deferred to his opinion. Bobby was most decidedly not in the least like Julietta.

Soon she was back, to inform him that her aunt would be joining them directly. She gurgled with laughter.

"My poor aunt! She swears I will be the death of her, and all because I have entertained you alone here for a couple of minutes! It is not respectable, she maintains, though what she thinks you might do to me in that short time with so many people within call, I cannot imagine!"

"My reputation has reached her, I collect," he said swiftly. "Or she may think I will carry you off for the sake of your fortune."

"Even though you have no need of a fortune," she replied candidly. "My father told me so little about his friends, so I knew almost nothing about your brother, just the fact that he was married at about the same time that my mother died."

"Yes. He was killed at Waterloo, and

left one daughter. He told me a great deal about your father, though."

Aunt Rose entered the room then, full of apologies for not being ready to receive the Earl, and voluble in her thanks for his kindness the previous night. He smilingly brushed aside her effusions, and rang for Betty to bring them the nuncheon she had prepared, cold meat, pies and fruit. After they had eaten Bobby competently organised her aunt and packed their dressing cases, and they drove round to Berkeley Square to find that their trunks had already arrived and had been unpacked. They were introduced to Mrs Chase, and then the Earl excused himself, saying that no doubt they would prefer to be left in peace and to dine privately, so he would be with them on the following day before his sister-in-law arrived.

Mrs Chase was a stout, gimlet-eyed woman, who smiled dutifully at them and led them, when the Earl had departed, to the rooms allotted to them. She thawed somewhat from her frigidity when Aunt Rose praised her housekeeping, saying how wonderfully brightly polished everywhere was, even though she had heard London servants were so unreliable. Soon they were deep in a discussion of the best ways of preserving fruit, and Bobby wandered from her aunt's room into the one adjoining which had been given to her. This one overlooked the Square, and she watched the busy scene outside, admiring the highly bred horses drawing the various fashionable equipages that were passing through, or bringing people to the houses.

Eventually Aunt Rose joined her, commenting that she thought they would be comfortable, for Mrs Chase was a very sensible body.

"The Countess will be more important," Bobby suggested, and then wished she had not mentioned that lady, for it put her aunt into a flutter of speculations about what she would think and say when she discovered the dreadful mistake that had been made.

Bobby grinned mischievously at her. "Well, I will not pretend that I have not often wished to be a boy! Life would be a great deal simpler then. But I do not think the Countess can do aught but accept it, and it is merely unfortunate, not tragic! Besides, the house belongs to the Earl, and he accepts us."

"Yes indeed." Aunt Rose was diverted. "What a charming man, though rather abrupt, I thought, to leave us so soon. I had quite made up my mind that he would dine here, even if he did not stay."

"I imagine he had another engagement, and thought it would be cosier for us to be alone until we are used to late town hours."

She sighed contentedly. Despite the initial misunderstanding, the Earl had welcomed them handsomely. Her first objective had been accomplished, and she was installed in London for the season. That was cause in itself for satisfaction, and she was aware of considerable excitement at the prospect of taking part in the social activities.

Briefly she recalled a letter from Jeremy that had arrived on the day before they had set out for London. In it he had made allusions to the following year in terms which implied that by then he and Bobby would be married. She frowned slightly.

Previously accepting the idea, she now felt more restless, less willing to bury herself in the depths of the country with Jeremy. Even this brief taste of London pleasures had unsettled her, she realised with some dismay.

Determinedly she dismissed these melancholy thoughts and concentrated on what was still her main task. In some manner she must discover the man Fitzjohn, and persuade him to explain to her the truth of the scandal that had so deeply affected her father. How ought she to approach the problem? She contemplated asking the Earl, or the Countess when she arrived, but came to the conclusion that this might be unwise, for they would wish to know why she was interested in the man, and it would be difficult to ensure that Aunt Rose was not apprised of her enquiries. Frowning, she admitted that she could do nothing immediately, but must restrain her impatience until she encountered Mr Fitzjohn himself, or found someone of whom she could make discreet enquiries.

4

ON the following morning Bobby dragged her not unwilling aunt with her to shop in Bond Street. Aunt Rose had been concerned not to be away from the house when the Countess arrived, but on consulting Mrs Chase she was assured that she need not expect my lady's arrival until late in the afternoon. Since Mrs Chase added some recommendations about the establishments her ladyship patronised, Aunt Rose became quite eager to go, and she and Bobby enjoyed a delightful couple of hours selecting a variety of gloves and stockings and slippers, as well as ribbons and laces and other gew-gaws. Bobby then espied the most dashing bonnet in the window of what Miss Holt had been told was one of the Countess's milliners, and insisted on buying it, despite the faint protests of her aunt when that lady discovered the shocking price.

"I have spent barely a quarter of my

allowance for years, Aunt Rose, so surely can afford to be extravagant for once," Bobby protested, and turned to discuss an alteration in the trimming with the milliner. When she had arranged for the bonnet to be delivered to Heronforth House she consented to return there herself, laughingly saying that her aunt no doubt expected her to squander all her fortune in one day.

"Of course not, my dear, but everything does seem to be shockingly expensive."

"London prices." Bobby shrugged. "You know some money was set aside for my coming out, and that I do not have to ask my trustees for it. There is ample to spend, and I mean to be in the first stare of fashion. It may be the only chance I have," she added, knowing perfectly well that this would reconcile her aunt to anything, and using the knowledge unscrupulously.

They returned to discover, to Aunt Rose's dismay, that the Earl had called and gone away again.

"Oh dear, how impolite he will consider us!" she exclaimed.

Bobby contrived to distract her by examining their purchases, and they were doing this when the sounds of arrival in the hall reached them. Aunt Rose was nervously of the opinion that they should wait in their rooms until they were summoned, but Bobby would have none of it, saying that they must at least introduce themselves to the Countess, and if they were in the way they could retire again. She bore her aunt off, and they descended to the hall where Shenstone, the Earl's butler, was supervising the unloading of a vast amount of baggage from a large travelling carriage that stood at the front door. Bustling about, giving directions that she immediately contradicted, was a small, fair haired woman in her late twenties. This must be the Countess.

Bobby advanced. "My lady?" she said enquiringly, and the Countess looked round, giving her a vague smile.

"Oh, I suppose you are the girl Dermot told me of. Really, you would expect him to get such a matter right at the start. He has not known you before, has he?" she added sharply, glancing in puzzlement at Bobby.

Bobby suppressed a smile. "No, my lady, and the mistake was partly mine for I did not think to mention that I was a girl. I thought it would be known. It was stupid of me, and I do beg pardon for any inconvenience it may have caused."

The Countess smiled. "Nonsense. Come into the salon and we can chat. Shenstone can deal with this without me for once, he ought to know where everything goes by now."

She swept away, and Bobby glanced at the impassive figure of the butler as she followed, surprising a look of relief in his eyes that caused her own lips to twitch in sympathy.

Inside the salon the Countess turned affably to them, and proper introductions were effected.

"James did tell me a few things about your father, but we had so little time together. He was away so often, fighting," she sighed. "I *warned* him what would come of it and said that in his position he ought not to risk his life, but he paid me no heed. It was surely enough for Dermot to be in the Hussars, without James going, but nothing would do for him but to become involved as well. Naturally he was the one to be killed, leaving me a widow, when Dermot had no-one to care whether he died or not!"

Bobby gave her an indignant glance, but Aunt Rose murmured sympathetically. The Countess smiled sadly, and went on to confide how very difficult she had found the task of bringing up her daughter while the child's father had been away so much, and after his death.

"Dermot simply spoils her," she complained, "so that she will pay no attention to what I say when he is around. He encourages her to defy me, I vow!"

After some time during which she dwelt on the miseries of her state, and Aunt Rose clucked sympathetically, and Bobby grew steadily more bored, the Countess decided that she ought to be supervising her maid, or else the girl would put things away in all the wrong places and never be able to find them.

"Do pray excuse me. Dermot left a message that he comes to dine tonight, though he does not intend to move in here for a day or so. It does make planning so much more of a problem for me!"

Briefly Bobby wondered when the Countess ever needed to make household decisions, for the house was admirably run, and she judged the servants more fully capable of arranging what was necessary than this somewhat vague creature.

Dinner passed off uneventfully, with the main topic of the Countess's conversation being a complaint that the Earl had avoided her house party.

"Julietta was not pleased, I could tell, though the dear girl is so sweet that she never complains."

She might be more interesting if she did, he thought, but he simply raised his eyebrows quizzically.

"I gave no firm promise, and as for Julietta, surely she came to see you, Sylvia?"

The Countess laughed archly. "Do not try to cozen us that half the girls in town are not hanging out for you!"

"Is Julietta one of these?" he asked swiftly, a gleam of amusement in his eyes.

"Julietta would not be so vulgar," the Countess replied haughtily. "She is my dear friend, though, and felt slighted after what was a virtual promise, despite what you try to pretend now. You did not have the courtesy to come, when she was expecting to meet you."

"Julietta can meet me very often in town," he replied, and then turned to Bobby. "I imagine you ride, Miss Blain? Will you wish to do so in town?"

"Indeed yes, I could not do without my horses!"

"Shall I mount you?"

She shook her head quickly. "Thank you, but my groom is bringing my own horse, Major, up to London for me. I would be grateful if you could recommend some stables."

"There is ample room in mine."

"But I wish to buy some carriage horses too."

"There will be room unless you intend to purchase a coach and six," he said laughing.

"Not precisely," she answered demurely. "If you do not object, then I would be very grateful. Can you help me to find a good pair?"

He looked at her and nodded. "I will

make enquiries. I believe I have heard of a suitable pair of carriage horses for a lady. I will see if they are still available."

Bobby opened her mouth to reply, and then thought better of it. The Earl's attention was claimed by the Countess, who had thought of a complaint about one of the grooms he employed at Heronforth Castle where she had been staying. By the time she had wrung a promise from the Earl that he would look into the matter, though Bobby noticed that he resolutely refused to agree to dismiss the man out of hand as the Countess demanded, it was time for the ladies to retire.

In the drawing room the Countess affably requested that they called her Sylvia.

"I feel sure we are going to be great friends, and it is so formal always to be 'my lady'," she said, "especially when we are living in the same house."

She went on to question Bobby about her riding, warning her that there were many dangers in town traffic that she would need to watch for.

"And do be careful about the driving pair you choose. Dermot has no idea of what are suitable horses for a lady to drive," she cautioned. "Do not be afraid to turn them down if you think they are not docile enough. I think a friend of mine means to sell her pair, and they would be far more suitable than any Dermot finds."

"Bobby is an excellent whip," Aunt Rose commented, innocently proud of her niece, but Bobby could see that the remark conveyed little to the Countess, who presumably considered that all females should drive at no more than a sedate trot. Bobby was thankful when the conversation passed to more domestic matters and her aunt could bear the brunt of it, which she seemed quite content to do.

On the following morning Bobby had just risen from her solitary breakfast, both the other ladies choosing to remain in bed, when Mr Fenton was announced.

"I came to see if you would care to drive with me," he said, beaming at Bobby, and admiring the pale green muslin gown trimmed with deeper green ribbons and flounces that she wore.

She turned to him in delight. "How kind of you! I should like that of all things. I will get my pelisse and bonnet at once!"

"Will you not need to ask your aunt's permission?" he queried, a little startled, and she shook her head.

"I am sure she will still be asleep, and in any event she would not refuse. I will leave a message for her."

She swept out of the room, and in a remarkably short time returned, the new bonnet perched jauntily on her curls. He led her out to his curricle, drawn by a pair of restive chestnuts, and handed her in. Taking the reins from his groom he set off at a smart pace.

Bobby looked about her eagerly, and George was kept fully occupied in answering her many questions. When they reached the Park Bobby expressed her admiration for the magnificent horseflesh they saw. Now their conversation was constantly interrupted as George was repeatedly hailed by acquaintances. He was forced to halt every few yards to introduce Bobby to his friends. These seemed legion, and although George was relishing the sensation they were causing, for everyone desired to discover the name of the unknown beauty driving with him, he rather regretfully realised that he had lost the opportunity for a long private conversation with Bobby.

At last they came to a less frequented part of the Park, and Bobby turned to George, her cheeks glowing and her eyes shining.

"I shall buy a curricle like this one, I am now decided," she informed him. "Can you direct me to a good carriage builder?"

George's eyes sparkled. Not many females drove such dashing vehicles, but he had Bobby's measure, and was willing to aid her in cutting a dash if that was what she wanted.

"Of course. I'll take you to my own, an excellent man. Now?" he suggested, and Bobby, delighted not to have to argue with him, nodded.

"That would be perfect, and if he has anything suitable, and I can find a pair of horses, I shall soon be driving them. A pair like that," she added, indicating a frisky pair of bays that were causing the driver of a perch-phaeton coming towards them some difficulty.

"You could hold such cattle?" George asked in some astonishment.

"Better than the cow-handed fool who has the ribbons now," Bobby replied shortly, and George gave a shout of appreciative laughter.

"Well, I think you might be in luck," he said. "I have heard that Fitzjohn is under the hatches."

"Who did you say?" Bobby interrupted sharply, hardly daring to hope that she had so soon encountered the very man for whom she had come to London.

"Percy Fitzjohn," George answered, glancing down in surprise at her tone. "Why so surprised?"

"I — I have heard the name," Bobby replied slowly, and then, improvising rapidly, "I had somehow gained the impression that he was a much younger man — if he *is* the one I have heard of."

"Most likely," George said, a little piqued that Bobby's attention should be distracted from him. "He's Dermot's cousin, so that is probably where you have heard of him. And as he's his heir, that could have made you think him younger.

But he's over forty, and they have little in common. Percy is one of the Carlton House set. He's been rather down on his luck the last few months; the cards must have been falling badly!"

Bobby began to perceive a way in which she might contrive an introduction to this man who held the key to her father's story.

"Do you think he might consider an offer for them?" she asked tentatively.

George grinned. "Those bays? Quite probably. I've heard he was considering selling some of his cattle, and if so, I'm sure he would be willing to let that pair go. They do not seem to be in perfect accord!"

"Could you make enquiries for me, discreetly?" Bobby asked. "I would like to meet him and try them out if there is any chance of buying them. I would rather not say anything to the Earl — or my aunt — until I have seen them closer," she explained, and George nodded understandingly.

"They'll try to dissuade you," he grinned.

Bobby smiled at him, grateful for his

willingness to become a conspirator, and they were in perfect charity with one another as George turned out of a gateway and drove her to inspect carriages.

To her great delight there was a curricle of exactly the type she wanted at the yard, and after some brisk bargaining which George observed with considerable appreciation, Bobby beat the man down to an acceptable price. She then requested him to paint it blue instead of its rather garish yellow, and said she would let him know when and where to deliver it. Highly satisfied with her morning, Bobby was driven back to Berkeley Square.

"I cannot thank you enough," she said as she bade George farewell.

He grinned down at her. "I want to see Dermot's face when he first sets eyes on you driving that outfit," he replied. "I will not say a word though, depend on me. I will see you tonight, for Sylvia has invited me to dinner."

Bobby spent some time later that day interviewing girls sent by the agency, rejecting most of them within a few minutes, but when she had almost despaired of finding a girl such as she wanted, she saw Eloise, a French girl of twenty, whose previous employer had recently died. Eloise seemed both sensible and gay, and had excellent references as to her proficiency in the various tasks of a lady's maid. She stated firmly the conditions under which she would agree to come, and this frankness impressed Bobby, for she had found most of the other girls either devious or obsequious when asked to state their views. She hired Eloise immediately, and had opportunity of being pleased with her choice that evening as the girl assisted her to dress for dinner.

Bobby was looking forward to this occasion with excited anticipation. She was interested in seeing how town manners differed from the only society she had ever known, that of small country squires and landowners who had few pretensions to elegance, and cared more for their acres and new methods of increasing the yield from them than for the latest *on-dits* or dictates of fashion. Sylvia had been vague when Bobby had seen her during the day, saying that as Bobby would know no-one there apart from the Earl and Mr Fenton, there was no need to stuff her head with all their names before she had need of them. In her rather distrait manner she had then fluttered away to give totally superfluous instructions to Shenstone, who had accepted them all blandly and continued to do as he wished as soon as she had nodded her approval and departed, to drive the Earl's chef to distraction with her suggestions for a different flavouring for one of his sauces.

"I am positive that Lady Whitmore said that her chef used rosemary, and I thought you would like to know," she said, smiling kindly at the little man, who stood there with his tightly clenched fists hidden behind his back, and his glance so downcast that his eyes were almost totally closed.

When the Countess departed, taking his silence for awed acquiescence, he exploded.

"Zat woman! Rosemary! To kill ze flavour zat is my own so carefully perfected secret! As for ze chef of ze Lady Whitmore, poof! 'E is a fool! I would not give 'is food to ze pigs! It would ruin ze bacon!"

"Since yer won't put it in nohow, whatever she says, I don't see no cause for fussin'," Mrs Chase commented tartly, her carefully refined accents of upstairs broadened to allow her native cockney to emerge.

"I shall go where my talent, my art, 'e is appreciated," Monsieur Henri stated grandly, bending over one of his pots and sniffing ecstatically.

"Don't pitch yer gammon to me. Yer won't find many so free with the blunt as 'is lordship, for the fancy messes yer makes so much commotion about!"

Mrs Chase, knowing from bitter past experience that she would not win any argument with the voluble little Frenchman, timed her exit carefully on these words, and when Henri turned to hurl a reply at her, she had disappeared. He shrugged, scolded the kitchen maid, who had listened in open mouthed awe at this battle of the gods, for some imagined misdemeanour, and gave his full attention back to his art.

His care was fully appreciated by

Sylvia's guests that evening, though it was perhaps as well that Henri could not hear Sylvia commenting on the excellence of the sauce, and confiding in her friend Mrs King that it was the rosemary that had made it so much superior to last time.

Mrs King and her husband had arrived first. She was a woman of Sylvia's age, and it transpired that they had come out the same season, and had remained on friendly terms. She was a pale, timid looking woman, who seemed perpetually anxious to agree with whatever the last speaker had said. If there was the slightest difference of opinion she kept glancing anxiously back and forth as though expecting those involved to leap suddenly at each other's throats. Her husband was tall and thin, with stooping shoulders, and considerably older than Mrs King. He seemed completely out of place in that gathering of people so much younger than himself, and made only the barest efforts at civil conversation, appearing to withdraw into his own thoughts most of the time.

The other man who arrived at almost

the same time as Mr Fenton and the Earl, was Lord Mapleton, slightly older than they were, and a friend of Sylvia's husband. Bobby took an instant dislike to him, for after greeting Sylvia and Mrs King, he had inspected Aunt Rose in a manner that caused her to dissolve into incoherence when he addressed her, and then passed on to Bobby, sitting beside her and paying lavish, fulsome compliments. When she responded coolly to his overtures, he leered at her, and spoke so that only she could hear.

"I knew your papa, my dear, in our first years on the town, so you may regard me as an uncle, and say just what you think, hey?"

"Indeed I shall," Bobby retorted, and he laughed in delight. Before she had time to elaborate more guests were announced, and instead Bobby seized the opportunity of escaping across the room to talk with Mr Fenton, although her mind was registering the notion that Lord Mapleton might, if he had truly known her father, be able to give her some information if Mr Fitzjohn was not the man she sought. She shuddered at the prospect of asking a favour from such a man, but however repugnant he was to her, she was determined to omit no action that could possibly assist her in clearing her father's name.

The new arrivals were a brother and sister, Paul and Julietta Howe. Bobby recalled the name as that of the girl Sylvia had mentioned on the previous evening, and she had realised that Sylvia was trying to promote a match between Heronforth and Miss Howe. She glanced across at the Earl to find him regarding her steadily. He smiled, then advanced to greet Julietta.

She was decidedly pretty, with fair ringlets framing a heart shaped face. Her eyes were large and soulful, and she had a habit, Bobby soon discovered, of opening them wide as she gazed attentively at the person she was listening to. Her features were delicate, and her figure slender but shapely. Her brother, a few years her senior, bore a strong resemblance to her, but he contrived to appear artfully windswept, his hair in careful disarray, and his cravat fractionally uneven.

"He thinks to rival Lord Byron,"

George said softly in Bobby's ear. "He even took to wearing heels of different heights, to induce a limp, until his friends laughed him out of it."

Bobby chuckled. "He can amuse me so long as he does not attempt to read his verses to me," she replied.

"You will be spared that for he holds, wisely no doubt in his case, that premature publication of his immortal lines would lower their impact, which I understand is to be devastating when it eventually hits the poor unsuspecting public!"

Dinner was then announced and Bobby, finding Lord Mapleton on her left, was thankful that George was her other neighbour. The food, as always when the renowned Henri was in charge, was excellent: the conversation was at times rather stilted, despite George's ebullient spirits and the Earl's polished ease of manner. Sylvia chatted away inconsequentially as did Mrs King, but both Mr King and Paul Howe seemed to prefer their own thoughts. Aunt Rose was overawed, and Julietta seemed content to wait until remarks were addressed to her, when she would smile and nod and gracefully agree with the speaker. Bobby tried to observe the Earl's demeanour towards her, wondering if he was of the same mind as his sister-in-law, but although he was attentive there did not seem to be any particular warmth in his manner towards her.

When the ladies retired Mrs King placed herself beside Bobby, and smilingly beckoned Julietta to join them, saying that such young girls would be good company for each other. It was the first opportunity Bobby had had of speaking with Julietta, and as Mrs King questioned her about her parents, saying that she had once met Robert Blain the year she had come out, and was horrified to learn of his early death, Bobby tried to include the other girl in the conversation. Julietta seemed perfectly content to listen, seemingly engrossed in Bobby's replies, and made no effort to respond. Bobby was decidedly relieved when the men entered the room.

George immediately came and sat beside Bobby, and Mrs King bore down on Aunt Rose, no doubt to continue her indefatigable questions. Seeing that Sylvia was talking to Lord Mapleton, and that the other two men were finding a common interest, unlikely though it seemed, in a book of prints, the Earl came across and sat beside Julietta who gave him a welcoming smile.

"I was about to suggest that we make up a party for Vauxhall," George said, turning to him. "Miss Blain will be interested, no doubt?"

"Yes, indeed I should. I have heard so much about it," Bobby said eagerly. "When can we go?"

"I like Vauxhall," Julietta contributed. "Do you recall the last time we went there?" she asked Heronforth. "It rained and we all had to shelter in one of the boxes. My bonnet was utterly ruined."

"Then let us hope the weather will be kinder on the next occasion. I will ask Sylvia to make up a party."

They were interrupted then by Sylvia who wanted to set up some card tables, and the rest of the evening passed with them playing cards. The Kings played brag with Sylvia and Lord Mapleton, but as Julietta protested that such a game was beyond her, the others had to be content with various round games of utter simplicity.

"One day will you play me at piquet?" Bobby asked George, hiding a yawn, for the pastime was neither exciting nor amusing.

Heronforth overheard her. "You are a gambler?" he queried, a quizzical look in his eyes.

"I think I have some skill, though I am sadly out of practice," she answered. "I played a great deal with my father when he was ill."

"I will certainly take you on," George offered willingly.

"I do not really approve of females gambling," Julietta said, smiling sweetly at Bobby, but she was looking at the Earl, and was disappointed when he did not offer to play with her as well. No doubt he agreed with Julietta, she thought disgustedly.

As the party broke up Sylvia drew Julietta aside for a moment.

"You must come and visit me in the morning, my dear. I have so much to talk about, and there has been no opportunity tonight. Also you can get to know Miss

Blain better, and help me entertain her."

Julietta willingly agreed, and then turned to bid Heronforth farewell, but there was a slightly anxious look in her eyes as she looked limpidly up at him. Julietta was by no means as stupid as she sometimes appeared, and she had spent a disquieting evening watching Bobby, admitting that she was very lovely, and calculating whether Heronforth was at all taken with this beauty who would be living in his own house, and therefore in a most dangerous position to upset her own plans regarding him.

So many girls had flung themselves in his way, and he had seemed to despise them for it, and soon lost interest in them. Julietta had shrewdly decided that she would attract his attention better by appearing sweetly aloof. She had made certain that she had become friendly with Sylvia, and was therefore frequently in the Earl's company, but she had demonstrated no particular preference for him rather than any other man, treating them all with flattering attention and docility. By the autumn of the previous year she had been hopeful that her tactics were succeeding, for Sylvia had marked her down as a suitable bride for the Earl. She had hoped to complete her capture that winter, during the time she was invited to stay with Sylvia in the country, but unaccountably the Earl had cried off his engagement to be present. Jealously she wondered how long Bobby had been known to him, and began weaving plans for showing Bobby in unfavourable lights. She must contrive to discover as much as she could from Sylvia the following day.

5

AT breakfast on the following day the Earl, who had now removed to Heronforth House, informed Bobby that he had arranged for some horses to be brought round for her to try out.

"I hope that you have no other plans, but naturally, if you have, I will send to arrange for these horses to be brought another day."

Bobby glanced across the table at him. "Are they quiet horses?" she asked demurely, and hastily dropped her head to hide her smile when Heronforth nodded.

"Indeed, ideal for a lady to drive," he replied, unconscious of her emotions. "They belong to the mother of a friend of mine, and she is having to retrench now that she is a widow. They are a reliable, steady pair."

"Otherwise you would not have selected them as suitable for me, no doubt."

He glanced at her sharply, struck by a slightly satirical note in her voice, but encountering her bland smile, thought that he must have been mistaken.

"Will you be ready at eleven?"

"As soon as they are here. I am longing to see them," Bobby said truthfully.

She left the breakfast room to go and change into a suitable dress, and reappeared wearing a smart pelisse with a high collar and four capes, and a jaunty little hat with a feather curled fetchingly round the brim. The horses had arrived and were being walked round the Square by a diminutive groom. The Earl led Bobby out and she looked at them, inoffensive but stolid animals, pulling a sedate looking phaeton, very different from the sporty looking curricle she had already ordered.

Her expression schooled to display serious attention, Bobby allowed herself to be handed up into the phaeton, and the Earl sprang up beside her.

"I will take the ribbons until we are in the Park," he said, reaching across to take the reins out of Bobby's hands. With difficulty restraining her indignant comment, she swallowed hard and then meekly agreed. He drove towards the Park and once inside, on one of the less busy roads, passed the reins to Bobby.

She had taken the measure of the horses at once, and had silently been castigating them as sluggish mules ever since. She was tempted to see whether she could startle them into improving their performance, but decided that it would do no good, and she would be wiser to reserve a demonstration of her driving skill until she had more worthy cattle to drive. So she kept them at a slow trot, making no attempt to vary the pace, and after one silent circumnavigation of the Park turned to Heronforth with a slight smile to suggest that they returned to Berkeley Square.

He was puzzled. She had made no comment, and having been used to his female companions making all sorts of comments, inane and sensible, on any horseflesh they encountered, he did not know how to deal with this uncommunicative companion. She did not offer the ribbons to him as they drove out of the Park, and as by now she knew the way back to his house, he sat back, watching her closely as she competently negotiated the traffic and brought the equipage to a halt outside his door. The groom ran to the horses' heads, though Bobby privately considered that they were the last ones likely to take any action on their own initiative, and the Earl handed Bobby down.

"Thank you for the ride," she said politely, and turned to go up the steps.

Heronforth stared after her for a second, then recollected himself and spoke to the groom. He caught Bobby up in the hall as she had her foot on the first stair.

"What did you think of them? Shall I make an offer on your behalf?" he asked.

She turned and smiled at him. "Oh, not yet, I believe. I do not care to make such a purchase in too great a haste. But I am most truly grateful to you."

Nonplussed, he watched her turn and mount the stairs, then went to the room which he called his study. Although there were several letters waiting to be written, he could not settle to them. He was intrigued. Until now Bobby's behaviour had been decisive and brisk, as when she had dealt with the swooning Miss Holt, and had immediately accepted the offer of his rooms. He did not believe that she would prevaricate over the purchase of a pair of horses. Also she was normally a lively conversationalist, but she had uttered the fewest possible words that morning. Perhaps she was feeling unwell. That must be the explanation, he thought, relieved to have solved the mystery of her behaviour. Strangely the idea disturbed him more than her silence had, and eventually he abandoned all attempts to settle to his business and went to try and forget Miss Blain by a session at the boxing gymnasium he patronised.

He missed Julietta by doing so, having completely forgotten Sylvia's remark the previous evening that she hoped he would remain at home for her visitor. Julietta had arrived just before Bobby had returned, and was found with Sylvia and Aunt Rose in the drawing room. Sylvia, exhausted after the dinner party, had her feet up on a couch and was regaling the others with a long catalogue of the iniquities of the servants at Heronforth Castle. She smiled vaguely at Bobby when she came in, asked briefly if she had enjoyed her drive, and carried on with her own recital without waiting for an answer.

Almost immediately more visitors were announced, and Bobby looked up, animated by surprise and some amusement, when Shenstone ushered in Lady Staple and Edward.

Lady Staple bustled in, apologising profusely for her unannounced arrival.

"We reached town yesterday, my dear Lady Heronforth, and I lost no time in coming to see you. I heard that my dear young friends here had found a haven with you. It was most kind of you to take them in."

She talks as though we were paupers, Bobby thought wryly, and turned to greet Edward. He was staring fixedly at Julietta, who fortunately was unaware of this steady regard, for she was being presented to Lady Staple. Bobby smiled and quietly spoke his name. He jumped, then turned towards her, his eyes gradually focusing on her.

"Welcome, Edward. I trust you are well?"

"Er, oh, yes, I think so. That is, delighted to see you."

He was rescued from his embarrassment by his mother, who called him to be presented to their hostess. At last he was introduced to Julietta and he bowed over her hand, holding it tightly as though he feared she might vanish while he stared at her in open admiration. She gave a slight laugh, not displeased, for she often had this effect on susceptible young men, and merely pulled her hand away from his clasp.

"You are a friend of Miss Blain?" she asked. "Are you in London for long?"

"Yes. The whole season. Mama does not usually stay. She says we must this year."

As though mesmerised he sat beside her, and since Julietta was not accustomed to lead a conversation, especially with a young man, normally only being required to accept their compliments, and smile and agree with the opinions they expressed, and Edward was virtually stricken dumb by his meeting with her, their dilemma afforded Bobby considerable amusement. She was herself sharing Lady

Staple's interrogation about why she had become a guest in Lady Heronforth's house, but since Sylvia chose to make all the answers, dwelling on her late husband's great friendship with Robert Blain, she had leisure to observe and enjoy Edward's clumsy attempts to engage Julietta in conversation.

Aunt Rose, anxious not to offend her neighbour, was quick to fill in any gaps left by Sylvia, and so Lady Staple was soon in full possession of the story, including all the misunderstandings. She turned to Bobby, smilingly shaking her head at her.

"My dear, I have always deplored your dreadful writing! Why, when you send me notes I can often scarce read them. But your father utterly refused to dismiss your governess, though I warned him that she was not suitable for a girl like you."

"My father thought otherwise," Bobby replied shortly. She had frequently had this argument with Lady Staple. Her governess had been extremely clever, but unconventional. It had been with real regret that they had parted with her when her own mother became ill and had sent for her. As Bobby, then fourteen, had vehemently opposed having a replacement, and her father had already known that he had only a few more months to live, he had agreed that she should continue her studies under his guidance, seeing in this an opportunity for them to spend more time together. When he had died a year later Bobby had declared that she could follow her own lines of study after that, and Aunt Rose, knowing that she would attempt to do all her father had expected of her, had agreed. They had both had to endure the strictures of Lady Staple on the matter.

Lady Staple smiled indulgently. "Bobby was always headstrong, Lady Heronforth. I wanted her to spend the season with us, but she would not have it. I suppose she had some nonsensical notion that her father had some claim on your poor late husband. If only she had consulted me, I could have put her right, but as matters have turned out I would be very willing to renew my offer. Will you not reconsider how very inconvenient your presence is here, and come to me, Bobby?"

Bobby smiled, with an effort. "Although

Lady Heronforth's husband cannot do as my father wished, she and his lordship have been kind enough to invite me here. That is as near as I can come to obeying my father's wishes, and though I thank you for your offer, Lady Staple, I must follow my father's wishes."

Recognising the implacable note in Bobby's voice, Lady Staple did not persist, but began to talk of mutual acquaintances. She was aware of Edward's absorption with Julietta, and thought this a hopeful sign. Either it would cause Bobby pangs of jealousy to realise that Edward was not her devoted slave, and this would incline her to accept the proposal his mother was determined he should make: or Julietta might be a better match, and then she would be free of the disconcertingly frank Bobby.

An engagement was made for all the ladies present to attend a party Lady Staple intended to give in a few days.

"I always do, to announce to my friends that I am returned," she explained. "It will no doubt be a shocking squeeze, but you will not refuse me on that account, I dare say. I shall look forward to seeing you there. Edward, we must take our leave, I fear. Goodbye, my dear Lady Heronforth. I will expect your brother-in-law too. And your brother, Miss Howe. I once met your mother, I will send her a card. Miss Holt, Bobby, I look forward to many pleasant occasions this year when we shall meet."

She eventually departed, taking a reluctant Edward away with her, and leaving the others momentarily speechless.

"Is she a great friend of yours?" Sylvia enquired. "I cannot recall having met her before, but I may have done, there are so many people, and I am so forgetful!"

"She does not often come to town, never before for the whole season, I think," Bobby replied. "She is our nearest neighbour, and Sir John was for long my father's friend."

"She can be rather dominating," Aunt Rose said apologetically. "The villagers are all terrified of her."

"Even the parson preaches what she tells him," Bobby said with a laugh. "I truly believe she would get up into the pulpit herself if he did not!"

Sylvia laughed uncertainly, a trifle

shocked. "I suppose we must go to her party. She is well connected, from what she said of her father's family. We must not offend her. Besides, she is your neighbour."

Bobby had been annoyed as well as amused by the visit, but they were all going to a ball that night, and she was able to forget her annoyance in her preparations for this event, when she expected to meet again many of the acquaintances she had already made in London.

After the dinner the chaise was brought round, and the Earl of Heronforth conducted the three ladies to the house in Grosvenor Square, where already long lines of carriages were gradually approaching the door to deposit their occupants under the awning that had been set up.

Immediately after she had been duly presented to her host and hostess, Bobby found Mr Fenton at her side complimenting her on the pale green silk gown she wore, and asking her for the dance that was just forming. He swept her away, and Bobby noticed

that Heronforth had quickly sought out
Julietta and was dancing with her. She
was smiling confidingly up into his face,
and he seemed amused by what she
had said.

"What is Julietta really like?" Bobby
demanded suddenly of George, and he
glanced down at her, amused speculation
in his eyes.

"Jealous?" he asked softly.

She stared at him uncomprehendingly
for a moment, and then laughed in
genuine amusement.

"I? Jealous? I take it you imply that I
have set my cap at Lord Heronforth? No
such thing, indeed! But it is clear Julietta
has, and I believe Sylvia encourages her.
What is she like? I have been unable to
get much conversation from her."

"Few people have," he returned dryly.
"Julietta is more willing to be thought
agreeable than to have her own opinions."

"I wonder if that would be to his
liking? I am certain he likes his own
way."

"Undoubtedly, but do not all men?"

She laughed, but shook her head.
"There are many who do, I grant. There

are others like Edward who wish only for peace, and to gain it do what their womenfolk demand."

"Who is Edward?"

"Oh, a neighbour in Dorset whose mother desires him to make me an offer. They have just arrived in London. She is no doubt fearful that I might escape her clutches if she is not here to watch over me."

She described the visit that morning, and he was laughing heartily as the dance finished and they stood to one side. The Earl and Julietta were nearby, and George could see Dermot watching them, but he did not approach, instead leading Julietta back to where her mother sat with the other dowagers on clusters of gilt chairs set at the far end of the ballroom.

By this time Bobby had been introduced to many young men, and she was soon besieged by partners. She thoroughly enjoyed herself, and found that she was being asked to go to many other parties, join expeditions, ride and drive, so that she wondered how it could all be fitted in.

George had claimed her for another

dance, and afterwards they had taken drinks out into the large conservatory situated behind the ballroom. There were a few other couples seated there, but as the next dance began and the music wafted through from the ballroom most of them left. After a while Bobby's attention was attracted to a couple seated opposite, in an alcove secluded from the gaze of people in the main part of the conservatory by bushy plants. The man, in his forties, Bobby judged, was eyeing them with some displeasure, obviously wishing them elsewhere.

"He's finding his pitch queered," George said in amusement, and Bobby grinned at him.

"Who is he?"

"Freddie Bull. He's got a small estate in Lincolnshire. Twice widowed, and by the looks of it angling for another wife."

Bobby looked at Mr Bull's companion. She was a pale, fair girl of about her own age, dressed in a pale blue gown that made her appear insipid. She was not looking at Mr Bull, but gazing abstractedly down at her hands that lay clasped together on her lap.

"Shall we give him his opportunity? Bobby, would you care to dance?" George suggested, and half rose to his feet.

Bobby had been watching the girl, who at that moment glanced across at them. Seeing George's movement a terrified look came into her face, and she cast Bobby a mute look of appeal.

"I'd prefer to remain here," Bobby said in a clear voice, and caught George's hand to pull him down again. "Can you not see she's in need of help?" she continued softly. "If they do not go in a minute, I intend to go and speak to them. Please back me up."

He raised his eyebrows and grinned. "As you wish."

"Have you any idea who she is?"

"One of Maria Sawley's brood, I think. There are about a dozen of them. I fancy this one was brought out last season, but did not take. Not surprising with such a fearful dragon of a mother. Her daughters will have to be exceptionally attractive to overcome the disadvantage of that as well as small portions."

"Poor child. I am determined to spoil his game. She is terrified of him," Bobby said with decision, and rose to walk across to the other table. Reaching it she smiled brilliantly at the ill-assorted couple. "Do pray excuse me, sir," she smiled at Mr Bull, then turned to the girl before he could reply. " I am certain I have met you before. Are you not Miss Sawley?"

The girl smiled tremulously. "Yes, yes, I am, but — "

"But you have forgotten me, I can see. It was at some country assembly, I am positive, not in London. Where can it have been?"

"We live in Hampshire," the girl said slowly.

"That is it! I am Bobby Blain, and have seen you either at Winchester, or just possibly Salisbury. May I sit down?"

She did so, oblivious of the cold disapproval of Mr Bull, and continued chatting to the girl who responded cleverly after her first surprise, showing considerable animation that greatly improved her looks. They chatted eagerly about acquaintances known to only one of them and George, watching the performance with appreciation, was not entirely convinced that they had never met before.

Mr Bull sat back with pursed lips eyeing Bobby with ill-concealed dislike. Realising that she was not going to go away, he at last rose, turned to Miss Sawley, and bowed formally. Bobby kicked George sharply on the ankle and he also rose, saying as he did so: "Will you honour me, Miss Sawley?"

Gratefully she nodded, and he held out his arm. Mr Bull, foiled, could do no other than ask Bobby to dance and she, stifling her unholy glee at the success of her tactics, smilingly accepted his arm and followed the others to the ballroom.

After that dance, Bobby was thankful to see that George had escorted Miss Sawley to an older woman, presumably her redoubtable mother. She herself was delivered to Sylvia, standing with a group of friends. As soon as he could escape her victim did so, and Bobby found his place at her side taken by the Earl, who was requesting the next dance.

"How did you meet that fellow?" he demanded as soon as he had led her away.

"Mr Bull? Oh, I introduced myself," she said airily.

The Earl stared at her in disbelief. "What in the name of heaven do you mean?"

She chuckled. "Ask George. We were in the conservatory, and he was there with Miss Sawley. She looked so desperate that I went across and pretended to know her. I must say she played up to me excessively well," she mused, "most girls would have said something stupid to give it away. But George got her away by asking her to dance, and Mr Bull had to ask me, though he was utterly *incensed* with me for spoiling his tête à tête!"

"Are you in the habit of interfering like that?" he asked, and she grinned at him.

"Oh, no, I am not a managing female, like Lady Staple. But the poor girl was truly distressed."

"Lady Staple? Is not that the visitor Sylvia had this morning?"

"Yes, and she was so annoyed that you had not been able to aid her in entertaining them. And Edward was blissfully happy just looking at Julietta!

Do you think him handsome, in a rather bold way?" she asked.

The Earl had already been told by his sister-in-law of the possibility of a match between Edward and Bobby, for Aunt Rose had not been able to resist hinting at Bobby's suitors. Now he looked down at her, trying to discern her feelings. He wondered if she could be jealous of the attention Edward appeared to have paid to Julietta.

"I have not had the opportunity of judging," he replied to her question. "Why do you ask?"

"I wondered if Julietta might like him," she answered, an abstracted look on her face, and he felt his heart contract at the realisation that she might love another man. Normally clear headed, and able to laugh at himself as well as others, he could not yet admit that this girl, erupting so unexpectedly into his life, had in a few short days done what no other had, and captured his heart. His thoughts were cut short, however as Bobby spoke again.

"Do you know Mrs Sawley? May I invite Miss Sawley to visit me in Berkeley

Square? I would like to know her better."

"I have met the woman, though I know little of her. Of course you may ask the girl if you wish. You are perhaps lonely?"

"No, there is so much to do. But I like her. Thank you. I will speak to her now."

The dance ended soon after that, and Bobby crossed to where her new acquaintance sat beside her mother. The Earl accompanied her and made it clear that the Sawleys would be welcome at his house, much to the older lady's gratification. She almost forgave her daughter for having contrived to put Mr Bull in a temper, though she did not know exactly what had occurred, for that gentleman had disappeared into the card rooms and her daughter had merely said that they had met a friend in the conservatory.

After chatting affably for a few minutes, the Earl drew Bobby away and led her to a secluded alcove, where he talked to her about her life in Dorset. She answered his questions readily, making light of the problems she had dealt with since her father's death.

"Aunt Rose was helpless, really, though she is a dear," she explained, and he silently agreed with her judgement, concluding that Bobby herself was not aware of how unusual it was for such a lovingly protected girl to be able to make the decisions that she took for granted. He found himself comparing her with Julietta, knowing that Julietta would never be so capable of acting on her own initiative.

Their talk was soon interrupted as Sylvia, on Lord Mapleton's arm, appeared.

"We wondered where you had vanished to," she said, shooting them a sharp glance, and with a note of censure in her voice. "Your aunt is looking for you, Bobby."

Heronforth smiled lazily. "I am sure Miss Holt must know that her niece will come to no harm in my charge," he drawled. "There can be no haste, and I will escort Miss Blain to her when we are ready."

Sylvia pouted. "You will never take my advice, Dermot, and it seems most odd in you to disappear with Bobby like this. People will remark on it."

"If they have nothing better to do."

"But I really ought to go, to prevent Aunt Rose from becoming too distraught," Bobby said swiftly, and smiled at Sylvia. "As for people gossiping, they must be great ninnies if they think that, living in the same house as we do, the Earl has to steal me away at a large gathering in order to be private with me!"

Leaving a speechless Sylvia, she walked off, and Heronforth had much ado to school his features into solemnity as he followed her. Bobby turned to him as he caught up with her.

"I am sorry! I should not have said that, but I have always spoken without thinking. Aunt Rose warns me that it will get me into trouble, but it is so ridiculous!"

"People too frequently are," he agreed. "They abhor plain speaking in others, possibly since they dare not themselves say what they would dearly wish to!"

She considered this. "If they think much at all," was her verdict.

They came to Aunt Rose, sitting with Julietta and her mother, and she smiled at Bobby, asking how she was enjoying herself. The Earl turned to Julietta and made some comment. Unobtrusively Bobby watched him, puzzled, for the better she came to know him the more she wondered at his apparent preference for Julietta. Was it simply her loveliness that attracted him, or her docility, or was there something else that she had not yet discovered, possibly something that appealed to men? Julietta seemed to have many admirers thronging about her, and Bobby recalled Edward's immediate enslavement. She concluded that most men, including, it seemed, the Earl, preferred a beautiful but empty headed woman to one that had ideas of her own. While Bobby knew that she was not a scholar, she was aware that she could never behave like Julietta. I shall not have to if I marry Jeremy, she thought, recognising that her cousin did not regard her in a romantic light, but probably accepted the idea that they would some day marry in much the same spirit as she did herself. The thought worried her, and suddenly the future looked bleak.

6

THE unaccustomed mood of depression had gone by the following morning, and Bobby was her normal cheerful self. When Mrs Sawley and her daughter were announced she welcomed them, and after a few polite words had been exchanged, left Mrs Sawley with Sylvia and her aunt and bore her new friend to the far end of the drawing room on the pretence of showing her some music.

"Thank you so very much for coming to my rescue last night," Miss Sawley exclaimed as soon as they were out of earshot.

"Was he being very unpleasant?" Bobby asked sympathetically.

"Yes." She shuddered. "Oh, Miss Blain, I cannot bear the idea of marrying him, yet Mama says I must if he offers. I was so afraid that he would do so last night!"

"Do call me Bobby. What is your name?"

"Celia."

"Well, Celia, cannot you refuse to accept him? No-one, surely, can force you into a match you do not desire. He does not look the sort of man a girl like you would wish to marry. Mr Fenton said he has been widowed twice."

"They were fortunate!" Celia commented with a faint laugh. "He has eight or nine children, and a son older than I am. Even if I liked him I could not face with equanimity the prospect of acquiring such a family!"

"Why is your mother so anxious for you to accept him, then? Is he wealthy?"

"No, a mere competence. But we are not rich either, and it is my second season. I had no offers last year, for I did not take. Mama says that if I do not receive an offer this year I must become a companion to an old aunt of hers. You see, there are four more younger sisters at home."

"The season has hardly begun. Is he the only likely prospect?" Bobby asked bluntly.

"I know of no others," Celia confessed. "I am not pretty, nor rich, nor lively. I almost fancy the position of companion will be more congenial than marriage to someone I dislike."

"Indeed, yes! It is abominable that we have to catch husbands or be considered failures, while the men can do as they please and attract no censure! But there might be an attractive curate, or a local squire at your aunt's," she suggested bracingly.

Celia giggled. "No! Not one. And if there were I should certainly never meet them! I was so deep in disgrace after last season that I was sent to her for a few months, so I am well aware of what it would be like. She never entertains, apart from a couple of other old ladies, and she has lots of cats! Cats! If they were dogs it would be more bearable, for at least I could take them for walks, but there is little fun in grooming cats all day long! Not even the cats appreciate it!"

Bobby laughed. "Something is bound to happen, and if it does not we will make it! You shall come to stay with me in Dorset. I do not know many people, but I am sure I could do better than your aunt! Oh, but I might be in

Cornwall," she recollected. "No matter, if I am married I can entertain more easily, and even in Cornwall there must be some eligible bachelors!"

"You are betrothed?" Celia asked a trifle wistfully, and Bobby shook her head.

"My cousin," she explained. "I expect I shall marry him in the end, but nothing is yet arranged," she added hastily, pushing away the thought.

They chatted, and Bobby wondered why Celia had not attracted admiration. She was pretty in a delicate way, and while she dressed in unsuitable, unflattering colours, that was probably her mother's doing. When she lost her shyness she could be a most entertaining companion. But most likely with Mrs Sawley's presence looming over her she did not often have the opportunity of abandoning her usual reserved manner. Bobby determined to try to detach her from her mother as much as possible, and in furtherance of this plan begged Mrs Sawley to allow Celia to take tea with her on the following afternoon, a request readily granted, for Mrs Sawley was well aware of the advantage of cultivating the friendship of such exalted personages who lived in Berkeley Square.

Later that day Mr Fenton came to ride with Bobby, for her own horse Major was now in London, and she rode him every day, usually in George's company.

"I have seen Fitzjohn this morning," George told her as they reined in after the first gallop.

"Is he willing to sell?" Bobby demanded.

"At a price. Unfortunately he was just leaving town for a few days, but I have arranged for you to inspect them as soon as he returns."

"Famous! I am so grateful to you. But pray do not tell Heronforth."

"Why not? Oh, do not fear, I will keep mum, but are you afraid he will forbid it?"

"He has no right to forbid me!" Bobby exclaimed vehemently. "No, I wish to surprise him, that is all."

For some reason she did not care to explain that the Earl had suggested some other horses for her, so she began to tell George about Celia, and fulminating against unfeeling parents who ruined their children's lives by taking no heed of their happiness. George, admiring her flashing eyes and animated expression, was fully in agreement. She turned speculative eyes upon him.

"Why do you not come to tea with me tomorrow?" she asked innocently. His eyes brightened, and then he paused in his reply to look at her suspiciously.

"When Miss Sawley will be with you?"

"Yes, but you need not mind that, she really is a pleasant girl."

"I am afraid I must refuse, there are — er — matters I must attend to, a visit to my tailor, in fact," George improvised swiftly but determinedly.

Bobby laughed, no whit put out that her scheme had been seen through. "Oh dear, I cannot be subtle and devious," she said ruefully, and he gave a shout of laughter.

"You will become a managing female if you do not take care," he warned.

"I know, and that I would detest, but when I see other people making such a muddle of things I cannot help *aching* to take over from them! I know that I would do it better!"

"Apart from trying to make a match for me."

"Yes. Sylvia says that you are a confirmed bachelor."

"Oh, does she?" he demanded, incensed that Sylvia should call him what he had always determined to be, just when he was contemplating changing his state.

"Worse than Heronforth," Bobby nodded, laughing at his indignant expression. "He is to be saved by Julietta, according to Sylvia's hints."

George laughed again, his good humour restored. "He will have to be in a sad state to offer for her, when he could have almost any female he wished for!" he commented.

"Why has he not married?" she asked curiously.

"He has been so busy avoiding the lures cast for him these ten years past that I think it has become a habit with him. I do not think he has ever met a female that did not bore him within a month."

"But Julietta would surely bore him," Bobby exclaimed.

"Indeed. And I cannot understand why he appears to treat her with so much more favour than the rest. Of course Sylvia has taken her up so that he can scarce avoid meeting her all the time, but I have sometimes wondered whether he is becoming tired of evading matrimony, and has decided to abandon resistance."

"It seems odd," was her only comment, and then she changed the subject, chatting about other people she had met until he escorted her back to Heronforth House.

Celia had been with Bobby for half an hour when another visitor was announced.

"Mr Jeremy Holt," Shenstone said portentously, and Bobby sprang up with delight to welcome her cousin.

"Jeremy! What in the world do you here? Why are you in town? I had no notion that you would be coming."

She then recalled her guest and presented Celia to him, firmly refusing to accept Celia's suggestion that she should go and leave the cousins together.

"Fustian! Jeremy can tell me why he is here, and then join us for tea. Shenstone will bring another cup. Why are you in town, Jeremy?"

"You are the same as ever," he observed. "I came up to town to do some business, and have decided to spend a week or so here. You always tell me that I bury myself down in Cornwall, so I am endeavouring to change my habits."

"By all that's wonderful!" she exclaimed, laughing at him unrepentantly.

They spent a gay hour then, Bobby describing some of the people she had met, while Celia, losing some of her shyness, contributed remarkably funny impersonations of some of the dowagers she knew, mostly friends of her mother. She had the trick of spotting and being able to exaggerate their foibles in an inoffensive way, and Bobby was convulsed with laughter as she recognised one aged Countess, who invariably poked her unwary listeners with her fan which, Celia solemnly informed them, had been especially strengthened so as not to break.

Jeremy watched in amusement, though he did not contribute much. When Celia's maid called for her and she left them, he turned smilingly to Bobby.

"I am pleased you have so swiftly made friends. Miss Sawley is most entertaining."

"I did not think she had it in her, for she is horribly repressed by that odious mother of hers," Bobby replied, and regaled him with her own description of Mrs Sawley and her wish to marry Celia off to the unpleasant Mr Bull.

"Parents usually know best," he replied agravatingly.

"Wait until you meet Mr Bull and his eight children!" Bobby said darkly.

"Eight stepchildren? For that girl to manage?" he said, startled.

"Oh yes, and one older than she is," Bobby informed him. "Is that what you would call a suitable marriage?"

"Well, I cannot know all the circumstances," he said judiciously, "but it seems to me distasteful, especially if she is averse to it."

"If!" Bobby exploded. "Can you imagine any girl of eighteen wanting to marry a widower — twice over — with so many children, and who, besides, is an ugly, pompous ass?"

"No, but you become rather too vehement, cousin. Let us change the subject. How is Aunt Rose?"

For a while they talked of family

matters, and then Jeremy rose and crossed to the window. He seemed ill at ease. After a short silence he turned and came back to stand beside Bobby, looking down at her seriously.

"Bobby, you know what Aunt Rose hopes for us, that we shall one day marry? I think the time has come. I had no notion that you wanted to spend the season in town, or I would have arranged to bring you for a time after we are married. I do not like the thought of your being beholden to the Earl of Heronforth."

Bobby stared at him in dismay. Although in the past she had half accepted the idea of marriage with Jeremy, now that it was suddenly presented to her she recoiled against it. Wildly she sought for excuses.

"I — Jeremy, I *can't!*" was all she could manage.

He sighed, looking at her remorsefully.

"I have been too sudden. Please forget that I spoke too soon. I propose to stay in town for a while, and I will see you often. You will become more accustomed to the idea."

Fortunately he then took his leave, but Bobby was very shaken by his proposal. Trying to examine her feelings, she could only surmise that she was enjoying her first taste of London society, and was unwilling to relinquish it so soon. Also, she had as yet made no progress in discovering what the story of her father's ruined reputation was, and she could not think of anything so important as marriage until she had accomplished that.

Impatiently she waited for the days to pass until she could visit Mr Fitzjohn, and eventually George called for her one morning, to drive her out, and said that they could try out the horses that morning.

He drove her round to Mr Fitzjohn's lodging in North Audley Street, and she was ushered into a cluttered sitting room. Mr Fitzjohn approached to take her hand, and offer some refreshment. She studied him with interest.

"Thank you, yes," she responded, much to George's surprise, for he had expected her to be anxious to drive the horses at once.

Fitzjohn was a man in his late forties,

of medium height and slim build. He was dark, but several streaks of grey gave his hair an unusually patchy appearance. His eyes were pale, and his colour unhealthy, heavy pouches of skin under his eyes bearing further witness to the irregular life he led.

"I understand you stay with my cousin," he remarked when he had handed her some wine.

"Yes, though it was his brother who was my father's friend. My father mentioned you occasionally."

Mr Fitzjohn nodded. "I met Robert Blain a few times," he said.

"I have met so few of his old friends, I am pleased to meet you, and hope we can one day talk of him."

He made a non-committal reply, and turned to George with a question. The conversation became general for a few minutes, and then Mr Fitzjohn rose.

"Shall I show you the horses now?"

He led her down to the street where his groom was waiting, the horses harnessed to a high perch phaeton. To Bobby's experienced eye the horses were showing signs of tiredness, and her lips curled.

Mr Fitzjohn did not wish, obviously, to deter a prospective purchaser by allowing her to see them in a fresh and possibly intractable condition.

Leaving George to await her return, Bobby allowed Mr Fitzjohn to hand her up into the phaeton, and then he clambered up after her and took the reins. They proceeded at a sedate pace towards the Park, and Bobby effusively admired their free action. Pleased with her praise, Mr Fitzjohn gave her the reins and Bobby concentrated on driving. She had to try out all their paces, to appear a plausible buyer, but it was with reluctance that she urged them into a canter, for they were tired. After a short burst of speed she allowed them to drop to a walk, and turned with a smile to her companion.

"They are sweet goers, Mr Fitzjohn. I would indeed like them. What is your price?"

"I thought four hundred," he replied smoothly.

Bobby had already seen the horses at their best, and had determined to buy them from him without this formality of a drive, but it had given her the opportunity of making his acquaintance. His price was far too high, but she dared not offend him, and she did not wish to make him aware that she was more knowledgeable than he assumed.

She hesitated. "It is really more than I can afford," she said regretfully. "Could you not lower it a trifle, for I am quite taken with them?"

"They are my best pair, but for you, my dear young lady, I will accept three hundred," Mr Fitzjohn replied, and Bobby almost showed her astonishment. He must be desperate to make a sale, she judged, and knew that if she cared to she might beat him down still further. But she wanted his goodwill.

"It is still more than I intended, but I will pay it," she agreed, smiling up at him delightedly.

As they drove back to North Audley Street they arranged that Bobby would bring the money the following day, and arrange for her new curricle to be delivered to Mr Fitzjohn's house so that she could drive it back in style to Berkeley Square.

"I'd wager the price you're paying me

to see Heronforth's face when you drive up in a bang up outfit like that," Mr Fitzjohn chuckled, and Bobby grinned. She was looking forward to that too, but for rather different reasons.

"Can you come before eleven? I want to drive out of town to visit a friend?" Mr Fitzjohn asked, and Bobby willingly agreed.

In the event her expectations were fully met. George walked with her to North Audley Street, she gave Mr Fitzjohn his money, and saw the horses put to in her own smart new curricle. Today the horses were fresh and she drove them round the park a few times to try out their paces properly. Satisfied, she then drove back to Berkeley Square and drew up outside Heronforth House just as the Earl emerged in riding dress.

"Good morning, my lord," she hailed him, for he had not even glanced at the curricle as he came down the steps and turned away to walk towards his stables.

He swung round at the sound of her voice, and stared in astonishment.

"What the devil do you do, driving

Fitzjohn's pair? They are his, are they not?"

"They were, but now they are mine," she informed him coolly.

"Yours? You mean that you have bought them from him?"

"I do."

"Of all the hoydenish things to do!" he exclaimed angrily, and Bobby's colour rose.

"Pray why?" she demanded.

"They are only half broke, that is why! They are dangerous, totally unsuitable for a female to drive!"

"But entirely suitable for a ham-handed man, I take it?"

He stared in silence for a moment. "There are many more suitable for you," he said mildly.

"Like that pair of sluggardly snails you would have foisted on me?"

"You think too highly of your abilities."

"But I have the advantage of knowing my skill, and you do not," she retorted. "Come, I will prove it to you! Mr Fenton, I thank you most warmly for your help, but would you now be so kind as to give your place to his lordship?"

136

"So you have aided her? I might have known it!" Heronforth commented to George, who had leapt down beside him.

"And see the reward I get, being thrown out as soon as you appear," George rejoined with a grin. "Thank you for the ride, Miss Blain. Pray do not upset his lordship in a ditch with your ham-handed driving!"

Bobby laughed, but her eyes were fixed on the Earl. He glanced from her to George and then, grim faced, jumped up into the curricle. She waved to George who stood and watched as she circled the Square and turned back towards the Park. Heronforth sat with arms folded, staring straight in front of him, and after one glance at his face Bobby refrained from commenting.

She drove towards the Park but did not turn into it, taking instead the turnpike that led towards the village of Kensington. Heronforth gave no sign that he had even noticed the direction they were taking. For a while the road was busy and Bobby had to concentrate on holding in the horses, but soon they had left the village behind and were out in more open country. She urged them on, seeing that there was another curricle ahead, and they needed no further bidding to produce their best pace and rapidly overhaul it. The driver glanced round, and seeing that he was being overtaken whipped up his own pair. Bobby let a low laugh escape her, and pulled her horses back slightly so that they held the crown of the road just behind the other vehicle. She stole a glance at Heronforth, but he was sitting as before, with his eyes half closed and an inscrutable expression on his face.

The road before them was straight but narrow. A post chaise was approaching them, and Bobby had to pull over towards the side of the road to let it pass, but the moment she was clear of it, seeing the road ahead empty, she drew out and urged her team on so that they drew level with the team in front. The driver glanced across and his mouth dropped open in astonishment. Bobby saw with amusement that it was her horses' late owner, Mr Fitzjohn, presumably driving his steadier horses on the visit to his friend.

His slight hesitation gave Bobby the

advantage she needed, for his horses had slackened their pace and she was able to sweep past with only a few inches to spare and pull over in front of him. He did his utmost to keep up with her, but his horses were not so fast and he could not maintain the pace she set. When she was well in front Bobby slowed down her team and seeing a small ale house ahead, pulled into the yard beside it to turn round and head back towards London.

As she was turning the horses, Heronforth still silent beside her, Mr Fitzjohn drew up in the yard.

"Well driven," he called to her, and then saw her companion. "Why, Dermot, I had not realised it was you. Will you not both join me in a glass of wine?"

"My apologies, Percy, but we must return, we came rather further than we intended."

"A pity. But we must have a proper race some day, Miss Blain."

"Indeed yes," Bobby agreed.

"We must go," Heronforth said curtly, and calmly took the reins out of Bobby's hands and set the horses in motion.

She sat silently for a moment, then,

when he had negotiated the turn into the road, reached over to retrieve them.

"Do you suspect I will spring them?" she enquired gently.

He smiled down at her, the grim look fading from his face. "No. I apologise, you are an expert whip. Though you must agree that few girls can drive so well."

"I was taught by my father."

"And you must have despised me for showing you the horses I considered suitable. Why did you not tell me then?"

"Would you have believed me?" she demanded.

"Touché. Probably not. But you can handle these cattle better than my cousin. How much did he sting you for them?"

"I paid three hundred. But why were you so anxious to leave him? The horses could have done with a rest, and he seems pleasant enough, apart from his driving!"

Heronforth frowned. "I do not choose to encourage you to frequent his company," he said shortly. "You are in a manner under my care, and Fitzjohn, despite being my cousin, is an undesirable acquaintance! He leads a disreputable life and is, besides, a gazetted fortune hunter."

"Over half the *ton* must be hunting the fortunes possessed by the others," Bobby observed, and a reluctant grin crossed the Earl's face.

"The other reasons are more important. I advise you to avoid him."

"I would prefer to choose my own friends," she replied mildly.

"I am well aware that I cannot force you to my view," he said seriously, "but to be seen in Fitzjohn's company would lower your reputation. It might frighten off some of the more eligible men."

She looked at him, startled. "Oh! Then you imagine that I am here to catch a husband?"

He grinned down at her. "Are you not? Then you must be the only female in town not so occupied!"

"You have an inflated opinion of yourself," she suddenly flared out. "You imagine every poor female is plotting how to ensnare you, and spend your time evading traps that exist only in your imagination! I had no need to come to London to marry Jeremy! Or Edward, for that matter, but I am in no haste to marry! I have something *far* more important to do here!"

He eyed her in amusement. "So you are different. Most girls, as I am sure you will admit, have little alternative but to catch the best husband they can, and many men consider that marrying an heiress is an honourable way to earn a living! No, do not frown at me so ferociously, it is unfortunate but true. Tell me instead what your other reason is?"

Furious with herself for having said so much, Bobby shook her head.

"I cannot. It — it concerns someone else besides myself," she said at last.

The Earl regarded her curiously, then began, with his usual urbanity, to talk of different matters, and they made the return journey feeling far better disposed to each other than earlier.

The Earl, however, was wondering in some perplexity what Bobby had meant when she had mentioned marrying Jeremy. Was she already promised to her cousin? He was as little suited to her as Edward Staple, Heronforth told himself, though so ingrained was the attitude of years that he refused to allow his thoughts to make the obvious step of deciding that he himself was.

7

THE next few days passed swiftly. Bobby saw Celia several times, and grew very fond of the girl. Away from her forbidding mother Celia blossomed, and several of the men who flocked around Bobby, and had at first wondered that she should select for a friend a girl who made no favourable impression on the *ton*, began to take an interest in Celia for herself.

Jeremy continued in London and Bobby saw him almost every day. To her relief he made no further attempt to propose to her, but by his attitude she realised that he considered the matter settled. Time enough to think about that when he mentioned it again, Bobby decided, reluctant to consider what it was she wanted. To her rather mischievous amusement Bobby watched Edward falling more and more under Julietta's spell. Lady Staple, having discovered that she had no more than a modest dowry, had turned her attention once more to Bobby, and was doing her utmost to stir jealousy in Bobby's breast. Bobby listened with unholy joy as Lady Staple regaled her with accounts of how she feared that Edward would lose his head over Julietta.

"For you must admit, my dear, that she is very lovely, quite enough to turn any man's head. And so delightfully tractable, an excellent quality that a man appreciates. Dear Lady Heronforth has implied that there is an understanding between her brother-in-law and Julietta. For myself, I think him too high in the instep. Julietta may well consider that a more homely man is better to her liking. She is very partial to Edward, as you may have noticed."

Stifling her laughter, Bobby thought of the way the two of them, Edward and Julietta, often sat without a word for minutes on end, unable to start a conversation. When Edward did manage to utter some commonplace remark, Julietta would sigh and agree, but she rarely offered any comment herself. Bobby had noticed, however, that on several occasions when the Earl had been present

Julietta would seem more absorbed in Edward, smiling on him more intensely, but glancing round from time to time to see how Heronforth was taking this.

So far as Bobby could judge he seemed oblivious, treating Julietta with the same politeness as before, but utterly unaware that he had a rival for her affections. He was either confident or uncaring, and she could not decide which. This, to her irritation, annoyed her. She admitted, reluctantly, that from the way most females treated him he might have every right to be sure of his power over them. Julietta never obviously pursued him, which might be why he liked her; but with Sylvia's efforts on her behalf she did not need to, having many opportunities of meeting him. Bobby doubted whether there was any understanding as Lady Staple thought, but she was fully aware that Sylvia was determined to do her utmost to make Julietta her sister-in-law.

It was at another ball that Bobby met Mr Fitzjohn again and he immediately approached her and complimented her on her driving.

"I would not have believed my cattle could have been so skilfully driven," he said generously. "My cousin Dermot did not appear to be enjoying the demonstration, though!"

"He did admit that I could drive," Bobby answered.

They danced, and Bobby led the conversation round to cards, mentioning that her father had taught her to play, and lamenting the few opportunities she had been offered of playing since he died.

Mr Fitzjohn regarded her consideringly. "Then will you take a hand with me now? The card rooms are quiet yet," he added, seeing her hesitation.

Bobby had immediately longed to accept, but she knew that to play with such a man in public would be considered fast. But it was true that she had played much with her father, and had scarcely enjoyed the silver loo and games of chance that Sylvia thought were the only suitable card games for ladies to indulge in. And it might be the answer to her problem of how to persuade him to tell her the truth about her father. The temptation was too great.

"Piquet? One partie?" she suggested, and Mr Fitzjohn, delighted, nodded agreement.

He called to a waiter to arrange a table, and supervised the setting of a candelabrum in a suitable place. The room was virtually unoccupied at this hour, but in the usual inexplicable way news of the game had spread and several of Bobby's friends came crowding in to watch and lay bets on the outcome.

"What stakes?" Mr Fitzjohn asked as he escorted Bobby to the table. "One of your curls?"

"If that is what pleases you," Bobby replied after a slight pause. "From you I would ask some information about my father."

He looked sharply at her, then slowly smiled and nodded.

They cut for deal, and Mr Fitzjohn won, giving him an advantage. He smiled in satisfaction and dealt the cards. Bobby found that she had a good hand and only discarded three cards, improving it with her new ones. On the points score she was ahead, and she just won seven tricks to draw further ahead on the first deal.

Then it was her turn to deal the cards to Mr Fitzjohn who became Elder Hand. She played steadily, concentrating fully on the game, so that she forgot the spectators silently watching the contest.

In the next four deals Mr Fitzjohn recovered the ground lost, and though Bobby played well, the cards were rather against her, so that by the time it came to the last deal Mr Fitzjohn was well ahead. She had the final deal, and refusing to give up hope kept a smile on her face as she did so. They picked up their cards.

"Ten for Carte Blanche!" Mr Fitzjohn exclaimed, and rapidly counted out his hand to demonstrate that there were no Court cards in it. Then he discarded five of the cards, picking up several that allowed him to gain extra points. Bobby had a difficult choice to make. In the end she made only one discard, and to her relief obtained a good one in exchange from the talon.

Bobby declared her hand. She held good cards and her score crept up, but she was still fifty behind her opponent. The only possible way she could win the partie was to take every trick and score an extra forty points for a Capot. She held three of the Aces, and her best hope was that one of the cards left in the talon was the remaining Ace, so that she could gain and keep the lead, hoping thus to make any high cards held by her opponent worthless.

The atmosphere was tense, the excitement round the table growing as the watchers realised that Bobby still had a faint hope of winning. She might, as Younger Hand, take the option of exposing the remaining cards in the talon, but when Mr Fitzjohn led with the King of hearts and she was able to take the trick with the Ace and gain the lead, she decided that there would be more value in keeping them face down, and neither of them knowing. He would have been certain to lead with an Ace if he had one, knowing that he could foil her Capot by taking just one trick. If he had the advantage of knowing those cards left in the store it might help him when he had to select cards to throw away after he ran out of the led suits.

There was scarcely any sound. Their breathing and that of the spectators was barely audible, and only the slight flick of the cards as they were laid down broke the silence. Bobby won trick after trick, leading with her two strongest suits. To her immense relief Mr Fitzjohn threw away the eight of spades that could have beaten her seven. But he might still have the nine. She had two cards left. Taking her decision she led with the other card in her hand, the Knave of diamonds, and almost showed her relief when Mr Fitzjohn, after a slight hesitation, threw down the nine of spades. Her seven then took the final trick and she had won the partie by a bare three points.

She looked up and took a shuddering breath. "I did not think I would do it!" she exclaimed.

"You are an excellent player," Mr Fitzjohn complimented her. "Your father was good and must have taught you well."

"My father! Yes, he was," she agreed slowly. In the excitement of the game she had almost forgotten the reason for it.

"I will pay my debt tomorrow?" he queried softly.

"I ride early in the morning."

Bobby, flushed with pleasure, then turned to receive the enthusiastic congratulations of her supporters as they crowded round her, then she espied the Earl of Heronforth, standing behind the crowd, and regarding her with cold disdain. She flung up her head and stared back at him, challenging his look as he approached her, seeming to carve a path for himself by some magic.

"My dance, I believe," he said coolly, and bemused, she allowed him to lead her away. He did not, however, take her to the ballroom. She passed through a door he held open for her, and found herself in a small parlour. She looked round at him unflinchingly as he leaned against the door and surveyed her sardonically.

Bobby took a deep breath. "Do we dance here?" she asked, annoyed and a little frightened of his mood, though determined not to allow him to realise that he could affect her in such a way.

"What do you mean by making such a spectacle of yourself, gambling in public on your skill at cards, and with such a fellow as Percy?" he demanded.

"What is it to you what I do?" she

riposted, aware only too well that her behaviour had been outrageous, but determined not to admit it, especially to him.

"It is important to me because you are my guest. I care not what madness you enter into, apart from the fact of that. In my brother's stead I am responsible for you. I do not care to see you embroiled with my disreputable cousin and his like."

"I shall choose my own friends, if you please!"

"I do not please. I have once before warned you that he is an undesirable acquaintance. But whoever it had been, from now you will be regarded as fast and the higher sticklers will avoid you."

"That concerns me not a button! I can do without their approval!"

"So you think. But what if vouchers for Almacks were refused? Many of the *ton* would then reject you."

"That would not concern me overmuch! But if you are afraid that my reputation will besmirch your family more than that of your cousin already does, I will remove to an hotel tomorrow! Now pray stand aside and allow me to pass."

He did not move as she approached
the door, and she halted, unsure how
to proceed. Rather to her astonishment
he suddenly stepped forward and took
her hand in his. Amazement kept her
motionless for a moment, and then she
attempted to slip away from him and out
of the door he had left clear. He was too
quick for her and caught her by the arm
as she passed him. Without thought she
raised her other hand and dealt him a
stinging slap across the cheek. Aghast
she stared at him and saw a light kindle
in his eyes. Both his hands were now
on her shoulders, and she fully expected
him to shake her, but after a minute of
immobility he dropped his hands and
turned away.

"I — I beg your pardon," she said,
fighting back the tears of shame that
were filling her eyes.

"I must rather beg yours," he replied
formally. "I have no right to make any
criticism of your behaviour."

"But I *was* behaving abominably!"
Bobby declared, a break in her voice. "I
realised it, but the devil was in me, and

there was besides a *very* special reason! Now I have made it worse and proved to you that I *am* a hoyden and do not know how to behave! I am so ashamed!"

To her astonishment he laughed. "You can take pleasure in the fact that few men have ever managed to plant on me so neat a hit," he told her, crossing to where she stood and pulling her round to face him. "We have both behaved in entirely uncharacteristic ways, so shall we grant each other the pardons we have begged, and forget it? Though I wonder if we have been merely behaving naturally for once, without the veneer of politeness the world imposes on us?"

She chuckled, sniffed, and glanced shyly up at him. It was all he could do to refrain from taking her into his arms, she looked so adorable. His face was close to hers, and Bobby was tremblingly aware of his immense charm as he smiled down into her eyes.

"I — I will not play again with Mr Fitzjohn," she said, unable to think of any other response, and his smile faded.

Dropping his hands from her arms he moved away. "I should not have said it, but he truly is not the right sort of person for you to be encouraging. Sylvia will not warn you, and as I am in some sort a guardian, I must. Until your Jeremy can relieve me of the responsibility."

"He is not my Jeremy," she retorted, angry at this assumption on his part, though when she thought about it afterwards she could not imagine why she should disown her cousin so vehemently, for she was eventually going to marry him, wasn't she?

The Earl ignored her protest. "Shall I be thought to be blushing in confusion if we emerge from this retreat?" he asked, turning his head so that the cheek she had slapped was facing her.

Bobby laughed. "It is almost faded, and I do beg your pardon," she said contritely.

"A salutary lesson I no doubt deserved," he said lightly. "But if it remains at all I must remain here, and I will keep you a prisoner until you cease repining on it. Who taught you to play piquet so well?"

"My father. I did have good cards in the last deal tonight."

"And skill, though I was in no mood to appreciate it. Will you play with me some time? In private!" he added swiftly as he saw the gleam of mischief in her eyes.

"I would be honoured, my lord," she responded demurely. "For pence?"

He raised his eyebrows quizzically. "I would prefer a different stake! Now I think I am in fit condition to return you to your aunt. I trust no-one has been seeking us."

"Before my reputation is quite ruined by my having been alone with you for so long," she said swiftly, and he laughed.

"Minx!" was all the reply he vouchsafed. He carefully opened the door and seeing that the coast was clear led her out and to the ballroom. He did not, however take her back to Aunt Rose, for the musicians were striking up a waltz and without asking her he seized her round the waist and swung her into the dance.

Bobby had danced the waltz before, but only a few times, for it was still considered very daring and not played often. She found herself breathless held so tightly and whirled round so expertly, and knew that part of her confusion was because it was the Earl who held her so closely. She had been treated to a good measure of his charm, and realised that he was having the same effect on her as on many other females. Angrily she berated herself for stupidity, telling herself that it was merely reaction to the distressing scene they had enacted earlier, and when the dance came to an end she parted from him rather brusquely when she at last reached the haven of Aunt Rose.

Sylvia was regarding her with some curiosity, and Bobby turned with relief to Jeremy who appeared beside her to claim her hand for the next dance.

"I am not sure that you ought to dance the waltz," he chided gently, and Bobby looked at him in annoyance. She had been subjected to enough argument for one evening, she thought angrily, and retorted that if the Earl of Heronforth, her host, considered it suitable then Jeremy need have no qualms.

"Maybe not," he said slowly, "but I would prefer that you used your own judgement. I have heard that he is rather a wild man at times. Why do you laugh?"

Bobby shook her head, overcome with

mirth to have her mentor himself castigated for the crime he had imputed to her.

"Miss Sawley refused to dance it," Jeremy continued, affronted by her laughter. "You could do well to take your lead from her. She has done the season before and is up to snuff, you know."

Bobby suppressed the uncharitable thought that it had not done Celia much good, for she was really fond of her, and was certain that any failure on Celia's part to secure a husband was more the fault of her unprepossessing mother than any lack of attributes in Celia herself. She managed to sooth Jeremy down, and turned the conversation onto safer topics. She was relieved that he did not appear to have heard of her card game with Mr Fitzjohn, for though she was ashamed of the impulse that had led her to accept his invitation at a large ball, she knew that any criticism from Jeremy would cause her to react angrily, and it had achieved the desired promise that she would learn at last what she wished to know about her father.

That ball was one which Bobby was thankful to leave. She slept badly, dreaming again of the Earl as she had the first night she had met him, but this time in the dream they seemed to be waltzing for ever. Early the next morning, with only her groom Shearer for company she rode out into the Park to meet Mr Fitzjohn.

There were not many of the fashionable crowd about yet, for it was only ten o'clock, and so Bobby was able to work off some of her restlessness by a long gallop. As she was returning, with Shearer a few paces behind, she heard her name called and reined in. Mr Fitzjohn was riding towards her and he gave her a friendly smile.

They rode silently for a time, and after another gallop had taken the edge off their mounts' freshness, Bobby slowed to a walk.

"The wager, Mr Fitzjohn," she reminded him gently.

He looked across at her, a crooked smile on his lips.

"Ah, to be sure. I am not at all certain that you will like the truth, Bobby. I may call you that, may I not?"

"You promised to tell me," she said

firmly. "I know not whether I shall like it, but I must know the truth."

He laughed. "Well, I am a gambler, and I pay my debts of honour. I have a suspicion what it is you wish to know. You have been warned."

Bobby detected a triumphant note in his voice, and she narrowed her eyes thoughtfully as she looked at him.

"You know the reason my father was accused of cheating at cards?"

"Indeed yes, for I was present when that game took place. Most of them, your father, my cousin James, and William Steer, are dead now. Only Dermot and myself remain."

"Dermot! But I understood that when this happened he was fighting in the Peninsula. At least — " she paused, " — he was there, was he not?"

"Not all the time," Mr Fitzjohn replied, watching her closely. "He came home on leave once or twice, and he was there. Just the five of us were concerned. Steer was one of Wellington's officers, also on leave from the war, and there was an argument. He claimed that he had been cheated — that the cards were marked, but he could not tell who was responsible. We examined the cards. They were marked, but so cleverly that it needed an expert to make use of them."

"Who could have done this?"

"The game took place at Heronforth House and the packs had been opened at the beginning of the game. It seemed obvious that James or Dermot had had the best opportunity, and Dermot had been winning heavily. But so had your father, and he was staying at Heronforth House."

Bobby was listening intently, her emotions very confused. She could imagine the Earl of Heronforth cheating at cards as little as she could her father, but after all, how much did she know of him? She had been his guest for a few weeks, and before that had not even been aware of his existence. How could she know what he was like! Her heart rebelled at the thought, but her clear mind advised caution. She must discover more.

"What happened?" she asked in a low, urgent voice.

Mr Fitzjohn shrugged. "Later that evening, when Steer had left, Dermot confessed. He explained that he had been very short of money — I believe there was some girl in Lisbon he was entangled with, a matter of paying off a promise of marriage — and had learned how to mark the cards from a fellow in his company. He was desperate, for if it became known he would have had to resign, and as a younger son had little income apart from his army pay."

Bobby, shocked and still only half believing this story, struggled to understand the implications.

"What of my father though?" she asked slowly. "Why was he blamed?"

"He had always been a good friend to my cousin James, though he barely knew Dermot, who was so much younger. James was frantic that the family name should not be dragged in the dust. They discussed it, and your father agreed to visit Steer, give him the money he had been cheated of, which James provided, and beg him to keep the matter to himself. This was done, but Steer talked, and as your father had been the one to pay over the money he was the one accused of cheating. The rumour gradually spread, and your father could not refute the allegation without involving James and Dermot."

"I see," Bobby said slowly, taking a deep breath. "And they were prepared to keep silence while he suffered?"

Mr Fitzjohn shrugged. "Dermot had returned to the Pensinsula and would not have heard immediately. James was newly married, and had always been careless of others. I went to him and protested, but he told me that your father had written to him, imploring him to say nothing since it would not harm him, he was no longer interested in society, and the scandal would die soonest if ignored."

"He would do so!" Bobby said, half proud of her father, half bitter at the thought of his suffering, and by now prepared to believe in Mr Fitzjohn's story.

"I blame myself for what followed."

"What else can there be?"

"Steer was home again, some leg wound. I went to him and in confidence told him that it had not been your father. I hoped that he could scotch the rumour, for no details were known, and Dermot would not have been harmed. He promised me to do his best, but the next I heard was that he had been killed. He had returned to duty, and there was some quarrel. It was hushed up, but Dermot was involved. It is clear to me that Steer went to him and accused him, and Dermot killed him."

"No!" Bobby protested in horror.

"I said that you might not like it."

"It is incredible, but it clears my father, and I cannot be other than thankful for that," she returned sharply.

They rode along in silence for a while, and then Mr Fitzjohn began to question Bobby about Lord Heronforth. It was soon obvious that he was concerned about the Earl's possible marriage. Bobby forced herself to drag her mind away from the fearful revelations she had just heard and answer his questions.

"He is paying an unusual amount of attention to Miss Howe," Mr Fitzjohn commented. "How does the wind lie in that quarter?"

"I have no information. As his cousin you are far more likely to hear before I do."

"Except that you are a friend of Miss

Howe, and Dermot does not, for very obvious reasons, like me! Before this happened, I often helped him out of scrapes, and wild young men do not regard older cousins who do this with fondness!"

"Naturally," she agreed, and then, to turn the subject away from the painful one of the Earl, she asked if James had also been wild.

"Why do you ask? James is dead."

"Curiosity," she replied. "He was my father's friend, and now that I know his wife I have been wondering what he was like."

"James was a fool, most of all to get himself killed," he said, so bitterly that Bobby was surprised.

"I do not suppose he wished it," she said mildly.

"He need not have ventured himself!"

This was almost the same view that Sylvia had expressed. They both seemed to resent James' death rather than grieve for him. In Sylvia's case, if she did not love him, this was understandable, for it had deprived her of a good deal of consequence as well as wealth, but why should Mr Fitzjohn, who had been brought one step nearer the title and the inheritance, be so bitter?

That puzzle was soon forgotten, however, and Bobby returned to Berkeley Square in a very disturbed frame of mind. Delighted though she was to have received confirmation that her father had not been guilty of cheating, and to know how his name had been blackened, the discovery she had made about the Earl had horrified her. It must be true, unlikely though it seemed, for Mr Fitzjohn had said that he had confessed. Not to the murder, she thought frantically, he could not have killed this man Steer! But why should Mr Fitzjohn tell her this unless it were true? He had no reason for lying about his cousin.

Having reached that conclusion, Bobby determined to leave Heronforth House as soon as it could be arranged. She knew that Aunt Rose would be perfectly willing to return to Dorset at once with her, and there was now no reason for her to remain any longer in London. She thought with a slight pang of all the gaieties she would miss, but then reminded herself that in order to partake of them she would have to remain at Heronforth House. There was no reason she could give except the true one, and she recoiled from doing that, to explain a removal to any other residence in London.

The prospect was bleak. It was not the thought of the country so much as that of leaving her new friends. She admitted to herself that she had come to depend on her new friendships, especially with the Earl, and the shock of the discovery of his perfidy had deeply saddened her.

8

BOBBY was unable to set in train her plans for returning home, however, for she found that Miss Holt had accompanied Lady Heronforth on a visit to friends, and later they were promised for dinner with Mr and Mrs King. The Earl was not to be found, and had his own engagement for the evening. Bobby reluctantly decided that she would have to postpone telling him her decision until the following morning.

She learned then, when she descended to the breakfast parlour, that he had driven out of town for the day.

"He had some business, Miss," Shenstone explained when she asked why he was not there. "He went early to be sure of returning in time for the party to Vauxhall."

Bobby had forgotten this entertainment, planned so long ago it seemed, and then lost amongst the many other pleasures she had been enjoying. It would be no pleasure now, she thought miserably, realising that she would have to endure it. The thought of going to Vauxhall in Heronforth's company, now that she knew what she did about his behaviour towards her father, was very bitter. In other circumstances she might have enjoyed it so much! Now it would be painful.

In an attempt to forget she had Major saddled and rode in the Park, where she was soon joined by Edward, who was riding alone.

"Good morning, Edward," she hailed him.

"Heronforth asked me to join the party to Vauxhall," he said abruptly, ignoring her greeting. "It is tonight," he said. "Who else goes?"

This was so typical of Edward that Bobby was amused, despite her former misery.

"Oh, I have almost forgotten. Let me think. Sylvia and I, and Heronforth, of course. George Fenton, and Jeremy, Celia and — " she paused, teasingly, and then took pity on the imploring look he turned on her " — and Julietta to be sure."

A smile spread over his face. "She's so beautiful," he said simply. "I've never seen anyone so beautiful."

This was almost lyrical from Edward. "Her brother was to have come too, but I remember Sylvia said that he might cry off. Some nonsense about struggling with recalcitrant rhymes, apparently," she explained but Edward had not heard a word. "You can thank Lord Byron for your inclusion in the party," she added tartly, and Edward, reacting to a tone of voice familiar from his friends, and especially from Bobby, paid her words some attention.

"Why, what did he say about me?" he asked. "Who is the fellow, anyway?"

Bobby cast her eyes to heaven, but did not attempt to enlighten him. "I will see you tonight, goodbye."

She rode away, feeling incapable of dealing with Edward's irrelevancies this morning, but he scarcely noticed that she had gone.

Back at Heronforth House Bobby was restless, wanting to leave, but unwilling to speak to Aunt Rose, who would certainly confide in Sylvia, until she had told the Earl himself.

Aunt Rose was in a flutter of apprehension in any event. Sylvia had come to find her soon after Bobby's return, to persuade her to join the party to Vauxhall, which she had earlier begged to be excused.

"I invited Lord Mapleton when Julietta's brother cried off," Sylvia explained. "Now it appears that Heronforth has asked Mr Staple. It is so like him not to consult me, but merely to leave a message! The numbers will be odd, so do please come. I am sure that you will enjoy it, even if you say it is for the young ones. You are not precisely ancient, after all!"

Bobby added her persuasions, thinking that the larger the party the less chance there would be of her having to talk with Lord Heronforth. In the face of their joint pleas Aunt Rose eventually capitulated, and spent the rest of the day with Bobby contriving a suitable trimming for the gown she intended to wear.

The guests were all to dine early at Heronforth House that evening, and as the ladies gathered in the drawing room to await them, Sylvia was looking annoyed.

"Has his lordship returned yet?" she asked Shenstone as he entered the room to receive some final instructions.

"Not yet, my lady, but he did say that he might be delayed," the butler replied soothingly.

"He deliberately chooses to be aggravating," Sylvia complained to Aunt Rose when Shenstone had removed himself. "Why he has to choose today to make some absurd visit into the country I cannot tell," she continued in an aggrieved tone. "I knew how it would be, that he would be late for this party he has insisted on my arranging! It is not as though Fitzjohn's business could not have waited."

"That is his cousin, is it not?" Aunt Rose asked, while Bobby was wondering what business brought the cousins together. Could Mr Fitzjohn be attempting to sell something to Lord Heronforth, she speculated.

"Yes, an odious man!" Sylvia replied. "He has always been a nuisance, and I never approved of James seeing so much of him. It was odd, because I did not think James liked him overmuch himself, but he always tolerated him. At least Dermot does not normally inflict him on me. I have that to be thankful for."

"Is he not the heir until your brother-in-law marries?" Aunt Rose went on.

"Unfortunately. There is no-one I would less like to see stepping into James' place."

Dermot's, Bobby silently amended, unconsciously using the Earl's name, and amused despite herself at Sylvia's bland ignoring of him and the fact that he had succeeded to her dead husband's dignities.

"Fortunately it is not likely to happen," Sylvia was continuing. "Dermot is at last showing signs that he plans to marry. Julietta is very amiable, is she not, and just the sort of wife for Dermot."

There was no time for more as the guests began to arrive. Sylvia was loud in her apologies for their host's absence, and cast George Fenton a look of annoyance when he laughed and said easily that no doubt Dermot would turn up before they had had time to miss him.

He did not, however, and Sylvia was obliged to confess that he had left instructions that they were to begin dinner without him if he were late.

"I do apologise on his behalf. We must begin now, or we shall be abominably late in arriving at Vauxhall."

Dinner was half way over before they heard the Earl arrive, and Shenstone unobtrusively slipped away from the dining room. A few minutes later he reappeared to say that his lordship would join them in a short while, but must change. Looking rather more wooden than usual he then spoke in a whisper to his most senior underling, and disappeared again.

It was a long time before the Earl came in, and when he did he had scarcely time to utter his apologies before Sylvia was enquiring what business had delayed him so long.

"I am sure no-one can be interested in such dull matters," he said repressively, and turned his attention to Shenstone who had followed him in and was hovering solicitously about his chair. "Just some beef, if you please, and burgundy. I must not delay us any more."

Bobby, momentarily forgetting her misery, was enchanted with her first view of Vauxhall gardens, the many walks among the trees and the carefully tended beds of flowers being illuminated with thousands of coloured lanterns. From the pavilion came strains of music, and the fashionable throng strolled about the walks, listened to the orchestra, or sat in the booths that lined the main avenues and where supper would be served later.

They went first to listen to the music which was enjoyable, though the standard was not particularly high. The musicians could be forgiven, however, for they played with great enthusiasm that affected the crowd and put them in a light hearted mood.

After a while they retired to the booth that the Earl had reserved for them, and watched the couples and groups parading before them. Then George suggested that they walked again, since it was some time before supper. Sylvia laughingly shook her head, for she had been deep in conversation with Lord Mapleton. Aunt Rose did not wish to go either, and the Earl chose to remain with them, to Bobby's relief. The other six set off to explore some of the side paths that they had noticed earlier.

Edward, not always slow, had hastened to offer his arm to Julietta, and since George was walking with Bobby this threw Jeremy and Celia together. When they had gone some way George slowed his pace so that the others drew ahead, and then whisked Bobby down a side turning.

"What is this?" she demanded, laughing at him.

He grinned, and put his finger to his lips. "Would you not wish to give Edward an opportunity to be alone with his inamorata?" he whispered conspiratorially, though since they were long out of earshot this was totally unnecessary.

"I cannot see Jeremy being so lost to all sense of propriety that he will go off with Celia and leave them alone," she commented.

"That is Edward's problem. I have done my best to aid him. Though I find him and his problems rather tedious, I admit. I would far rather talk about my own."

"Oh? I was not aware that you had any."

"No, for I hide a breaking heart under a gay exterior!" he responded mournfully.

Bobby laughed, though wondering a little bitterly whether the description could be better applied to her.

"That I cannot believe," she returned as lightly as she could.

"It may not be precisely true, Bobby," he said, serious now. "Though I do not allow my feelings to be displayed they are none the less real. Oh, confound it! I have never offered for a girl before and I am not a good hand at it! Bobby, I love you. Will you marry me?"

She stared at him in utter surprise and dismay.

"Mr Fenton, I had no notion! Oh lord, I sound so missish! But I *truly* had no idea that you regarded me that way!"

"Now you do. Bobby, you do like me, I think? Could you possibly consider marrying me?"

Slowly she shook her head. "I am sorry, but no. I do like you, I find you very good company, and exceedingly kind, but that is not love."

"Many marriages with less than that are successful," he pointed out.

"I know, and I thought, not so long since, that I would be content with that," she responded slowly. "I do not know why I have changed my mind, but since I have come to London I have! I think that a marriage may be successful, as you say, without love, but that would be only a partial success. I am determined not to marry until I can love and be loved also. I — I am fond of you, truly, but I know that I could never feel more towards you, and knowing that it would be wrong to even consider it. I am most deeply sorry!"

He stared at her for a moment, then smiled ruefully. "I swore I would never marry, unless the need for a fortune drove me to it! Then I fall in love like any green girl! It would be my ill luck to love you when you do not care for me. And no thought of your fortune ever entered my head!" he finished, attempting a laugh.

Bobby put out her hand apologetically, and he caught it in his, then lifted it and kissed it gently.

"The night you arrived at Dermot's

rooms, I had been saying to him that he was unlucky at cards, but lucky in love," he said softly, and she threw him a startled glance. Before she could speak, however, he went on: "If you ever change your mind, even if you do not love me, but want some haven, for heaven's sake do not allow maidenly modesty to prevent you from telling me!" he implored. "I promise that I will not plague you with repeated offers, but it will be open to you until you choose some other more fortunate devil!"

"Thank you, George. I cannot say how sorry I am, but I will not, so do not hope! But I would like still to be your friend."

"Crumbs from the feast! Your friendship will torment me every day," he responded, with some of his usual mocking gaiety returning to his voice.

She laughed, shakily. "Then must we part for ever?" she retorted swiftly.

"No indeed, that would be a worse fate! I can always console myself with the thought that females are notoriously volatile!"

"And men soon forget!"

He shook his head. "Shall we go and look for the others?"

They walked back the way they had come in silence. When they reached the wider path where they had left the others there was no sign of them, and so they set off in pursuit. At the end of that path there were smaller paths branching and they tried each of these in turn, without success.

"They may have gone back," Bobby suggested. "Were we very long?"

"It seemed an eternity! They are not likely to have returned so soon, and besides, they would have been looking for us. We can try some of the side paths further back."

They walked on, and soon saw Jeremy and Celia turn out of a side path ahead of them. George called to them and they halted, waiting for the others to come up. Celia was looking rather uncomfortable, and Jeremy refused to meet Bobby's eye, but she did not notice their discomfort, for her own thoughts were chaotic.

"Where are the others? Have they gone back?" she asked.

"No. I do not think so. That is, we

have not seen them. I mean that we lost them."

"You mean that they gave you the slip," George laughed. "Sly dog, Edward! He has more ingenuity than I thought."

"We ought to find them, it must be almost time for supper," Celia reminded them.

"We will take the paths on this side, and you look along the others," George was directing them, when Heronforth appeared behind him.

"We thought you lost," he said cheerfully. "Supper is almost ready."

"Edward and Julietta do appear to be lost," George informed him, watching his face closely for any signs of annoyance.

Heronforth merely glanced at him in amusement. "How did you come to mislay them?" he queried lazily.

"We were about to separate and look for them," Jeremy contributed hastily.

"An excellent notion."

He joined George and Bobby, and they trod along one of the less brightly illuminated paths. It ended in a wider space where another path joined it, and a rustic bench had been placed. As they turned into this open circle they saw before them the missing pair. Julietta was standing with her back to them so that they could not see her face. She had her hands set against Edward's chest and was looking up at him, and as the others appeared they saw Edward put his arms about her and clumsily pull her towards him, bending his head as he did so to kiss her.

Julietta moved her head aside, and Bobby heard a faint protest come from her. Before she could decide what best to do the Earl strode across the intervening yards and grasped Edward by the collar of his coat, heaving him away from Julietta.

"How dare you treat Miss Howe so discourteously," he demanded in a furious voice such as Bobby had never before heard him use.

Startled, Edward swung round and wildly attempted to hit his adversary, but Heronforth released him and with a light punch to the jaw sent Edward staggering back into George's arms. George promptly grasped him by the elbows but Edward, recalled to his senses, no longer struggled.

Julietta, suddenly released from her amorous swain, had looked about her quickly and then, seeing Edward disposed of, gave a loud sob and collapsed into Heronforth's arms.

Bobby looked from George, restraining Edward, to the Earl, supporting Julietta, and could not forbear laughing. It was in part reaction against the turbulence of her emotions and the strains of the last two days.

"Edward, you fool!" she gasped in between her laughter, and George seeing that he was no longer likely to resort to violence, released Edward and joined in her laughter.

"Have you no pity for Miss Howe?" Heronforth's cold tones cut across their laughter, and Bobby looked at him quickly.

"Lay her down on the bench," she advised, "she'll soon make a recovery."

Heronforth did so, with some relief at being rid of his encumbrance, George thought, observing him closely. Bobby bent over Julietta's prone form and whispered something in her ear. Julietta's eyelids flickered and then she moaned.

"Oh, what happened?" she asked faintly.

"Edward lost his head, though I do not see that having been rescued from his embraces should be cause for swooning," Bobby replied tartly. "Cause for celebration, I should have thought!"

Heronforth, seeing that Julietta had revived, turned to Edward.

"Your behaviour towards one of my guests is contemptible! If you cannot refrain from forcing your attentions on unwilling and unprotected females you had best not show yourself in my house again!"

Edward stared miserably at him. "I did not. That is, I thought — I didn't mean harm," he stuttered.

"No doubt *you* have never been swept off your feet and stolen a kiss when provoked," Bobby interposed angrily, coming to Edward's defence as she saw his abashed expression.

Heronforth turned towards her, his expression harsh. "I hold you to blame also for deserting Miss Howe and putting her into this unfortunate situation."

Before Bobby could regain her breath

after this attack, he had turned solicitously back to Julietta and was enquiring if she felt able to return to Sylvia.

"Oh, yes, please take me back," Julietta pleaded, clinging to his arm as he bent over her.

"George will take you back," he replied, and helped her to her feet. He handed her over to George before either of them were fully aware of his intentions, and jerked his head at George, who took the hint and bore off the faintly protesting Julietta.

"As for you, Staple, I would advise that you endeavour to make your peace before Miss Howe is regaling my sister-in-law with her grievances."

Edward, galvanised into action, realised the sense of this and made off after the others.

"Where are the other two?" Heronforth enquired, and Bobby started, for she had completely forgotten them.

"Looking for that precious pair," she answered shortly. "I collect Julietta escapes all your displeasure by shamming a swoon?"

He looked at her in surprise, and she surveyed him mockingly.

"I have no idea how Edward contrived to get her alone, but since she is older than I am, I take it ill in you to hold *me* responsible for her predicament. She is quite capable of dealing with Edward. If she cannot then she ought to be wary of enticing men with her sweet agreeableness! You will admit that she did not swoon so artistically until you were free to catch her," she added, and set off along the path with the intention of finding Jeremy and Celia. "Shall we look for the others, as everyone else is occupied?" she asked, and on receiving no answer, glanced back over her shoulder.

Heronforth was seated on the bench lately occupied by Julietta, and had slipped off his coat. To Bobby's horror she could see a patch of blood spreading rapidly over the upper part of his left shirt sleeve.

"What is it? Edward could not have wounded you?" she gasped, forgetting her anger with him and running back to kneel beside him. "Here, let me do it."

She ignored his protests and swiftly rolled up the sleeve, realising that there had been a bandage about his arm which had slipped, causing the wound it had covered to open and begin to bleed again.

"It is only a slight flesh wound, but I disturbed the bandage when I pulled him away from Julietta," Heronforth explained, watching Bobby's intent face as she competently tucked up the sleeve and rolled the bandage.

"We need some more linen for a fresh one," she said briefly, pressing the old bandage against his arm to stem the flow of blood. "Hold this tightly."

He obeyed while she swiftly pulled up her skirt and tore a strip from her petticoat. She tore off the lace that edged it, made a new pad and substituted it for the old bandage, then used the rest of the strip from her petticoat to bind it firmly in place.

"There, I think that is holding, and will bleed no more."

She rolled down the sleeve and considered the stain on it.

"I could bind some more strips of linen round that, which would stop the blood from staining your coat, I think, but you might not then be able to get your coat sleeve over the bandage."

"Tear out the sleeve. We can contrive to attach the cuffs to the coat sleeve in some manner," he suggested, and she nodded in appreciation, carefully arranging it and then helping him on with his coat.

"How did it happen? When?" she demanded, sitting down beside him at last.

"On the way home tonight. I was held up on Hampstead Heath by a highwayman," she said shortly.

"Did he steal anything?"

"No, and I fancy he is in worse state than I, for my aim was better. I got him in the leg," he said calmly.

She laughed rather shakily. "Who bandaged you up? It was well done, and would not have moved if you had not hauled Edward about."

"Shenstone."

"So that was why you were so long coming to dinner. But why keep silent? You need not have come here."

He shook his head. "I had no desire to ruin the party and it is a mere scratch. Will you keep my secret?"

"If you wish. Provided you absolve me

189

from blame in leaving Julietta alone!" she added swiftly, glancing speculatively at him.

He gave a shout of laughter. "I do apologise, but since you — since you are staying at Heronforth House, I am afraid I thought of Julietta as your guest too. Was she really shamming?"

"Of course! Though she almost succeeded in fooling me too. She only just stopped herself from opening her eyes when I whispered that there was a spider just above her head."

"You wretch!" He looked at her in amusement, and she suddenly felt unsure of herself and afraid. She glanced round: they were entirely alone. She recalled what she had discovered about him, that he was completely without principles, untrustworthy, and, if Mr Fitzjohn's insinuations were true, he had killed a man who might betray him as a cheat in cold blood.

"We had best hurry back," she suggested, standing. The Earl rose and offered her his uninjured arm.

"And hope that your cousin and Miss Sawley have not lost themselves. How was it," he continued as they walked along the path, "that it was Miss Sawley who contrived to be alone with Mr Holt and not yourself? Has the girl more cunning than I realised, and are you encouraging a traitor in your friend?"

Bobby swallowed nervously. "I was with George," she said in a low voice.

He shot her a swift glance, but her head was bowed and he could not see her face.

"Have you broken his heart too?" he asked lightly, and felt her stiffen beside him.

"Is not that Celia?" she asked hurriedly, pointing along another path.

It was not, and they reached the booth where supper was about to be served to find that the others had all gathered there.

"Dermot! You aggravating creature! I send you to find the others and you appear to get lost yourself!" Sylvia exclaimed in annoyance when she saw them.

"Yes, I did indeed get somewhat lost," Heronforth replied, and turned to speak to the waiter. Bobby slipped as unobtrusively as she could into a seat beside George, hoping to escape Sylvia's notice, but it was not to be.

"Why have you been so long?" she demanded, and Bobby glanced up to find Julietta's gaze, hard and direct for once, fixed upon her.

"Miss Blain tore her lace," Heronforth interposed smoothly, and Bobby looked up at him in dismay. "Someone had trodden on her hem, and she had to attempt to repair it. But the rent was too large, and she had to remove a strip of lace. I have it safely," he added, holding out his hand and in it the lace Bobby had so heedlessly torn from her petticoat and then forgotten. She reached out to take it, thinking that he must have retrieved it before they had started back, when she had been so intent on bandaging his arm.

"Thank you, my lord," she murmured, and took it from him. His eyes held an inscrutable expression for a moment, and then he turned with a light remark to Edward, who had been sitting in comparative safety next to Aunt Rose, but wondering miserably if his sins were to result in his banishment from the party. It was evident that the Earl had no such intention, and Edward relaxed. Julietta seemed to have entirely recovered and was listening to Jeremy's account of how he had contrived to increase the yield of his barley acreage over the past two years.

Celia was also listening, a rapt expression on her face, and Bobby recalled Heronforth's suggestion. Could the girl possibly have fallen in love with Jeremy? The idea startled her, for she had never regarded Jeremy in any romantic light. She admitted, however, that he was a fine looking, if rather stolid man, and with his farming talk he appeared safe and dependable, just the qualities Celia might admire. If it were indeed so, then she was pleased for her friend, but she wondered how Jeremy felt. He gave no indication, and yet it must have been Jeremy who had caused the two of them to become separated from Edward and Julietta. She could not imagine Edward with the wit to contrive that, although he had the audacity to take advantage of the sudden opportunity, she thought with a smile.

Realising that George was unusually silent, she turned to him, suddenly remorseful. He looked at her closely for a moment, then smiled reassuringly and began to chat about inconsequential matters.

Supper was served, and though several members of the party were having cause for embarrassment, it passed successfully. Afterwards they again strolled to listen to the music. The Earl was paying particular attention to Julietta, Bobby considered, watching him as he walked beside her, his dark head bent towards her fair one, apparently deep in conversation. Bobby followed with George, and they stopped a few paces from the Earl when they reached the pavilion. George was about to comment on the music, when a man to the side of him stepped backwards and cannoned into him.

"What the devil! Fitzjohn! Can you not look where you go, man?" George demanded wrathfully, but Mr Fitzjohn did not appear to hear him.

Lord Heronforth did, however, and turned round to look at his cousin.

"Well met, Percy. I fancy you do not

often come to Vauxhall?"

Mr Fitzjohn made some inaudible reply, and then hastily bowed himself away, still giving George no acknowledgement that he had even seen that he was there.

"I apologise for my boorish cousin, George. I fancy he must have received a shock of some sort," Heronforth said, and then turned to answer a question from Julietta.

"Looked more as if he'd seen a ghost," George remarked, and then forgot the encounter as he recognised another of the strollers and began to tell Bobby an amusing story about the man.

9

HEAVY eyed after a sleepless night, Bobby went to the breakfast parlour determined to ask the Earl for an interview that morning, and to tell him of her decision to leave. She had berated herself for not having taken the opportunity the previous evening at Vauxhall when she had found herself alone with him, but the shock of discovering that he was wounded had driven her own problems out of her mind. Or had she been too frightened, she wondered unhappily, remembering the feeling that had overwhelmed her as she had realised how alone and isolated they had been.

To her indignation she found that once more Heronforth had eluded her. Once again Shenstone informed her that his lordship had left town early.

"He went to Heronforth Castle, miss, saying that he had some urgent business there," the butler explained.

Bobby frowned. "How long will he be

away?" she asked.

"I cannot say for sure, miss, but for several days. He said that he was unsure how long the business would take."

Bobby finished her breakfast gloomily, wondering whether to abandon all idea of making an attempt to see the Earl, and simply to go home without seeing him. She was oddly reluctant to take such action. She did not see how Mr Fitzjohn's story could be untrue, but she passionately wished that it could be. She shrank from confronting the Earl with the accusations, but had come to realise that the only way she could possibly discover if they were true was to tell him and give him an opportunity to explain his side of the story. If there could be any other explanation, she thought in despair.

To distract herself Bobby had her curricle and pair brought round and drove herself to the Park, but her pleasure in the horses and the curricle was dimmed by the thought that soon she would be leaving London, and that it really would not be appropriate for her to keep them at home in Dorset.

Arriving back in Berkeley Square, her

own mood unlightened, she discovered Sylvia fluctuating between annoyance and satisfaction.

"Did you hear that Dermot had gone rushing off to the Castle?" she demanded as Bobby entered the drawing room.

"Shenstone told me," Bobby answered briefly.

"Aggravating creature! He tells no-one his plans until the very last minute, and then he disappears, leaving me a note only. I collect he fears to consult with me first in case I should dissuade him from going on these wild starts."

Privately Bobby considered that it was more to avoid recriminations, since Heronforth would never allow Sylvia's lamentations to influence his behaviour, courteous and considerate as he always was in the face of her unreasonableness.

"I understood from Shenstone that he had business there," Bobby said hoping that the subject would be finished. She should have known Sylvia better.

"Oh yes, and I have my suspicions as to what that may be," Sylvia replied, casting Bobby a triumphant glance. When Bobby did not reply, and seemed not to have noticed the look, she continued in a falsely sweet tone. "No doubt you can guess too! When a man, long a bachelor, finally decides to change his state, there are usually many alterations he needs to put in train at his houses."

Bobby looked at her, controlling the dismay that had smote her at these words.

"Did he tell you that was why he was going?" she asked bluntly.

Sylvia smiled, like a cat that had stolen the cream, Bobby thought dismally.

"No, no, my dear, but then he would not have done so in a note, which was all the communication I had with him. There was no need, however. You cannot have failed to notice the attentions he paid to Julietta last evening. She contrived to whisper, as she drove home with me, that she expected to have news for me in a few days. Julietta is not the sort of girl to raise her own or my hopes falsely, so he must have given some indication."

Bobby wondered fleetingly if Julietta had confided in Sylvia that Heronforth had appeared furiously angry when rescuing her from Edward's incpt embraces, then decided that there had been no time. His reaction then, however, and after supper, when he had devoted his attention almost exclusively to Julietta, could mean what Julietta implied. And he might have said something to her. If Sylvia's guess about the reason for his visit to Heronforth Castle was correct, then it seemed highly likely that he would soon be offering for Julietta. Bobby was unable to dwell on this thought, since Sylvia had reverted to her normal tones of complaint when speaking of her brother-in-law.

"He might have said when he was returning, instead of simply telling me in his note that it would be three or four days, depending on how long the business took. Now I shall not know whether he will be here for Lady Staple's ball the day after tomorrow! It is typical of Dermot to totally ignore my arrangements in this manner. He has no consideration!"

Bobby had forgotten the ball, which she had been looking forward to before the discovery of Heronforth's perfidy had swept it from her mind. Lady Staple had invited the reluctant Bobby to several events already, which she had dutifully attended, seeing no way of avoiding them without offending her neighbour. This ball, however, was different, because it was to be a masked affair. Bobby had not previously been to one, and hoped, under the protection of her mask and domino, to be free of Edward's reluctant attentions and able to enjoy the party more than she usually could when Lady Staple was preoccupied in throwing her and Edward together.

"He could have contrived to finish his business and drive up that day in time for the ball," Sylvia continued.

Bobby thought that the quarrel with Edward at Vauxhall might be a very good reason why the Earl would not return in time for the ball, though she did not think it explained his disappearance. He would wish for no open break because of the scandal, especially if he was to marry Julietta, but he would be likely to avoid all but the most necessary contact. Considering it, she came to the conclusion that if the actions of the lovesick Edward had offended him so deeply, he must be determined on marriage with Julietta.

"He may yet come," Bobby replied

soothingly, but Sylvia was not to be mollified.

"My numbers for the dinner will be out," she went on, undeterred by Bobby's apparent lack of interest. "And Julietta has such a charming dress she was planning to wear. I know she would wish to keep it for some other occasion if he is not present."

Bobby glanced across at her. "I do not imagine it will be entirely wasted," she commented. "Who else dines here before the ball?"

"Oh, Lord Mapleton and Paul Howe. There were to be just the six of us attending the ball, as your Aunt declined."

"Has Mr Howe completed his poem then?" Bobby asked in surprise, since that had been the reason for his not attending Vauxhall.

"He will have to come, to escort Julietta, since Dermot cannot be relied on," Sylvia rejoined pettishly. "I care not if his wretched poem is finished or not!"

She continued complaining in the same strain for some time, and it was with relief that Bobby turned to Shenstone when he announced a visitor. It was with surprise, however, that she heard Mr Fitzjohn's name. He had never before come to Heronforth House while Bobby had been living there, and she had gained the impression that he would not be a welcome visitor.

Sylvia also seemed surprised, but welcomed him graciously.

"We do not often see you, Percy."

He greeted her and smiled at Bobby.

"A fault I will endeavour to correct! It seems an age since I saw you, Sylvia."

He made polite enquiries after her and her daughter, then there was a short uncomfortable silence.

"Is Dermot at home?" he asked abruptly.

"No, he had business at Heronforth Castle," Sylvia answered, surprised.

"He — he is well, I trust?"

"Yes, indeed, and I think you will have a surprise soon, will he not, Bobby dear?" Sylvia said archly, smiling in what Bobby thought a most detestable way across at her.

She did not answer, and after staring at her for a moment Mr Fitzjohn went on to talk of a mutual acquaintance. The burden of the conversation was eased slightly when Miss Holt appeared, but she had very little to contribute, and it was a disjointed series of unconnected remarks. Mr Fitzjohn enquired solicitously of Bobby how her horses were behaving, and at last, conversation failing dismally, he rose to leave.

"Since Dermot is not here I must call again. I wished to see him on a family matter," he explained. "When will he return?"

"In a few days. I cannot be more precise since he did not inform me," Sylvia said aggrievedly. "Was it important?"

"Oh, no, not in the least. I will call again, but I hope to see you all at Lady Staple's ball? Dermot will not be there, I take it?"

"I cannot say. But I was not aware you knew Lady Staple?"

"Oh, I met her son a day or so back, and he issued me an invitation," Mr Fitzjohn explained, and at last made his farewells and took his departure.

"Well!" Sylvia exclaimed, almost before he was safely out of the room. "What in the world brought him here?"

"He does not usually visit does he?" Bobby asked. "He seemed most ill at ease."

"He used to come when James was alive," Sylvia told her, "but he and Dermot have never got on. I never could understand what James saw in him, he is a detestable man, and I cannot bear the thought of his getting the title if aught should happen to Dermot."

"Nothing is likely to," Miss Holt said calmly.

"No, and he will soon be married, I have no doubt. Poor James, if only he could have foreseen what I would have had to deal with I cannot imagine he would ever have gone into the army! I did not know what his family was like before I married him!"

Aunt Rose murmured sympathetically, and Sylvia turned to this much more responsive and satisfactory audience for her complaints. She seemed in the mood for confidences.

"I met his parents, of course. They were both delightful, and so kind to me. IIis mother died soon after the wedding though. She had never been strong, and she developed a fever which eventually killed her. It was fortunate that it did not happen before the wedding and delay that!"

"Poor woman, not to live to see her grandchild," Aunt Rose sympathised, while Bobby thought cynically that it was typical of Sylvia to be concerned solely with her own convenience.

"The old Earl did not live long after. He was much older than his wife, and had always adored her. Her death finished him. And, naturally, James had it all to deal with, for Dermot did not come home from the Peninsula. He left it all to James. I remember thinking then what a heartless creature he must be, for he wrote that as they had died and he could not see them, it was pointless for him to come to England, and his work in the army was too important to leave unnecessarily!"

"I am sure that having you to support him must have been a great help to your husband," Aunt Rose said comfortingly.

Sylvia smiled slightly. "That was about the one time that Mr Fitzjohn was of any use," she commented slowly. "He was older than James and knew a great deal about the family affairs. He had been a great friend to my husband before we married, and did assist him in settling up his father's affairs. James would have been willing to allow him to continue using Heronforth House when he was in London, as he had when the old Earl was alive, but I would not have it. I considered him a bad influence. He led James into undesirable company, and was a confirmed gambler, always in debt, it seemed. James considered my wishes to some extent, and though he gave up gambling himself, he would not entirely give up seeing Percy."

She went on to complain about the present Earl's inconsiderate behaviour, regaling Miss Holt with the story of his latest desertion and uncertain return. Bobby, who had been puzzling over Mr Fitzjohn's visit, even wondering if he had wished to see her alone for any reason, and had been foiled by Sylvia's presence, had been only half listening to Sylvia's monologue, and now withdrew entirely into her own thoughts.

Her reflections were not very cheerful. She had herself considered Heronforth's anger towards Edward a trifle excessive, and she was inclined to think Sylvia's prediction, that he would soon be making an offer for Julietta, was likely to be correct. It was somehow a distressing thought. Resolutely she pushed it and the implications from her mind, and forced herself to listen to Sylvia again, and join in the discussion of their plans for the next few days, though she had no notion of when or how she proposed to leave Heronforth House.

After what seemed an eternity she was able to escape, and in the privacy of her own room she could dwell on the thoughts she had suppressed earlier in the drawing room. Honestly she tried to determine why it should matter to her whether Heronforth married Julietta or not, and at last she admitted to herself that she loved him. Despite the account of his behaviour towards her father, which she was forced to believe, she loved him. She had not at first recognised the emotion she had felt as love, and since the revelations made by

Mr Fitzjohn had been fighting against the idea, feeling instinctively that she ought not to entertain such feelings for a man who had betrayed her father, and might even be a murderer.

Now, unhappily, she accepted that her love could not be denied, but vowed that he would never know of it. However much she loved him she could never bring herself, in the unlikely event that he offered for her, she interposed wryly in her thoughts, to be so disloyal to her father as to marry Heronforth. Then why should she care so much at the thought of his marrying Julietta? She will not make him happy, she whispered in agony. Anyone would be preferable to Julietta! It was not jealousy, she firmly assured herself, but the thought that he would soon be made exceedingly unhappy with such a wife, who could offer little apart from beauty and a placid acquiescence. That would never satisfy so vital a man as Heronforth, Bobby was sure.

Somehow Bobby got through the rest of the day, and the party Sylvia took her to in the evening. Fortunately none of her close friends were there to remark on her downcast looks. Aunt Rose, worn out with the effort of constantly sympathising with Sylvia, had pleaded a headache and retired early to bed. Resolutely Bobby refused to take this way out, much as she wanted nothing better than to bury herself with her misery. She was heartily thankful when at last she could escape.

By the following morning Bobby had concluded that she could not leave Heronforth House until after Lady Staple's ball, in order not to offend that lady. And after Sylvia's hints if she went now it would be regarded as a rout by Sylvia and Julietta. That she could not bear. She must see the Earl and after that nothing would matter. If he had no explanation, she must believe in his wickedness, and if he could in some miraculous way explain it, then she would not wish to go. Then she recalled that he might be marrying, and shrugged. At least she would choose her own time, and not be hustled away by hints from Sylvia.

Briefly she considered going for a ride, but as she was expecting Celia to come and spend the day with her there was not really time. She sat in the parlour she normally used and tried to read a book, but soon threw it down impatiently. Then she set out a game of patience, but gave it up when it did not work out. It was with relief that she turned to Shenstone as he entered the room.

He smiled paternally at her. All the servants approved of young Miss Blain, who knew exactly what she wanted and was determined to obtain it, but never made any unreasonable demands on them, as Lady Heronforth did.

"Your cousin desires a word with you, miss," he announced, and Bobby expressed her delight at this welcome interruption of her tedium.

"Thank you Shenstone. Jeremy! I am so pleased to see you, for I cannot settle to anything!"

Jeremy looked embarrassed rather than gratified by this welcome, and walked across to the table, standing with his back to her as he idly gathered up the cards lying there.

"Well, was it anything special that you came about, or a social visit merely?" Bobby asked him after a minute of silence. He swung round to face her.

"You are enjoying this London visit?" he enquired abruptly.

"Of course," Bobby answered after a moment's hesitation, unwilling to confide in her cousin. Suddenly, noticing his solemn air, she was afraid that he meant to renew his proposal. This she knew she could now never accept, however it might have simplified the situation. She knew too much of what she wanted from marriage ever to be content with Jeremy.

"I can see that you are very popular," he declared. "Have you — that is — I do not know how to phrase this without giving offence, but — have you received any offers? Oh, I realise that I am not your guardian and have no right to ask," he hurried on, "but I have a most particular reason for wishing to know. Have you?"

Bobby stared at him, observing that he was exceedingly ill at ease.

"I do not object to your knowing that I have," she answered slowly, "but I would prefer not to mention names, if you please."

He looked at her, relief plain in his eyes.

"I knew that you would! I was afraid that you might prefer one of the town beaux to me! But now, if you do, I shall be — that is, Bobby, although we have had an understanding that we would one day marry, would you care very much if I asked you to release me from my promise?"

"This is the reverse of an offer, I am to understand?" Bobby asked, amused and doing her utmost to keep the laughter out of her voice.

"I knew you would not like it!" he said miserably.

"Jeremy, there may have been an understanding, but it was not on *my* part," she said gently. "I never considered myself promised to you. It was a suggestion only, mostly Aunt Rose's, I think. When I was younger I accepted it, for most marriages are arranged by parents, but I have, especially in these last few weeks, come to realise that we are perhaps unsuited."

He listened, a mixture of relief and disbelief in his expression.

"You are brave and noble," he muttered. "I feel so despicable in asking it of you!"

Bobby could no longer keep her countenance. "Oh, Jeremy, do not be so mutton-headed!" she adjured him, laughing. "I am not brave at all, for I cannot love you, and indeed would consider it a *penance* to be forced into marrying you!"

He looked startled, and then somewhat offended. Bobby went to him and laid her hand on his arm.

"Pray do not mind me, Jeremy! I am fond of you as a cousin, but not as a husband. Is it Celia?"

He turned startled eyes towards her. "How — how did you guess?" he stuttered, and Bobby had to make a great effort not to allow her laughter to convulse her again.

"It's been plain to me for days that you were head over heels in love with her. Have you spoken to her? Does she return it?"

"Indeed I have not spoken," he replied in shocked accents. "I could not say a word until I had obtained release from our promises."

"There was no promise, but if there had been I would willingly release you, and I wish you well with Celia. She is a dear girl, away from her mother. I imagine you will be fully capable of dealing with *her*!"

"Indeed I shall. If Celia does accept me, we will live far enough away for her not to interfere, and she will in any event be fully occupied with bringing out Celia's sisters. I cannot presume, though, and think that Celia will accept me."

"I am convinced she is fond of you," Bobby said bracingly. "But you can put it to the test in a few minutes, for Celia is promised to me here. I will leave you alone. Unless, that is, you prefer soft lights and music? Shall we arrange another visit to Vauxhall?"

He looked shocked, but did not demur at her suggestion of leaving them together, and when Celia was announced a few minutes later, cutting short his rhapsodies on her perfections, Bobby soon contrived an excuse and whisked out of the room. Having calculated that half an hour ought to be sufficient time for Jeremy to come to the point she then returned, to find the lovers seated hand in hand, ready to overwhelm her with apologies, thanks, and praise of her unselfishness.

"Not in the least," she insisted. "I wish you both well, and I am certain, Celia dear, that you will be a *far* more suitable wife for Jeremy than I could ever have been, though he will not believe me when I say that I could never have been induced to marry him!"

Celia looked aghast at the thought that any female could have withstood the prospect of marriage with her adored Jeremy, and then became lost in contemplation of her own good fortune. Bobby was suddenly tired of their ecstatic conversation and somewhat curtly suggested that they might be better occupied in seeking out Celia's parents. Celia, afraid that her friend was after all hurt by her swain's defection, nervously agreed, and Bobby hastened their departure as quickly as she could without giving offence.

When they had departed Bobby went to find Aunt Rose and impart the news to her. As she had feared, the fond aunt was dismayed at the overthrow of all her plans, but to her credit, was far more concerned at Bobby's disappointment. She would not be convinced that this was non-existent, and spent the rest of the morning bewailing the ill fortune that had fallen upon them.

"It is what I feared when you made this mad plan to come to London," she cried. "Jeremy did not like it, and has seen you flaunting yourself in town, behaving wildly, and has naturally taken a dislike to it. I am surprised that a girl you befriended should treat you so badly, though, and would really not have thought it of Celia!"

"Aunt, dear, I would never have married Jeremy, so there is no cause for repining," Bobby repeated patiently. "As for Celia, she could not help falling in love with Jeremy, or stop him loving her! She did nothing disloyal, and I will not have you suggest it."

"Oh, you are so brave and generous, to forgive them and hide your sorrow! Would you wish to go home, my dear? No-one would think it odd in you! Do let us go home!"

Bobby almost laughed. She had been frantic to leave London until a few hours ago, and now the defection of Jeremy, and the expected triumph of Julietta gave her two very potent reasons why she must not.

"Of course not, Aunt. That would be the very *worst* thing to do. All the gossips would then say that I had been jilted, and had crept away to lick my wounds! That would be utterly false, and it would be hurtful to both Celia and Jeremy, spoiling their pleasure. No! I will not go home until it suits me, and that cannot be for some time."

Reluctantly Aunt Rose accepted this, but later, to Bobby's inward fury, insisted on praising her fortitude to Sylvia and Julietta, who was spending the afternoon at Heronforth House.

"How strange that Mr Holt should prefer that poor dab of a girl to you, Bobby. He has very odd tastes," Julietta commented insincerely. She had always been rather resentful that Jeremy had taken no more notice of her than civility demanded.

"I thought at first that Mr Staple was also one of your suitors," Sylvia said, smiling with false sympathy, "but even he does not visit here so regularly as he did."

She glanced meaningly at Julietta, but the latter seemed totally unaware of any hidden meaning. Certainly no blushes indicated that she recalled the incident in Vauxhall Gardens, and Bobby wondered whether Sylvia had been informed of that.

"Wild horses would not drive me into a marriage with Edward," she replied with a laugh. "As for Jeremy, there was never any understanding between us — on my part at least, so I cannot see what all the fuss is about. For my part I am happy for him and Celia. They will deal together excellently, and she will make him an excellent wife. I wish them happy, and trust that you all do too."

Bobby nonetheless had to endure their further comments, which she did with admirable restraint, for it was unrealistic to suppose that they could forbear discussing this development. When she finally escaped she was so brusque with her aunt that Miss Holt was convinced she was concealing a breaking heart.

10

THE next morning Bobby was riding early in the Park with only Shearer for company. When they dropped to a walk after the first gallop, the old man drew alongside her and glanced at her speculatively.

"Narrow escape for his lordship," he commented offhandedly.

"What do you mean?" Bobby thought that news of the highwayman's attack had reached the servants, and was not especially eager to discuss it.

"Yesterday," Shearer continued laconically.

This made Bobby pay close attention.

"Yesterday? What happened? Where?" she demanded, and Shearer, who had watched her progress with the various gallants she had ridden and driven with, and had his own shrewd ideas, smiled aggravatingly.

"He's not hurt, Miss Bobby, don't be afeard. It was at this Castle of his, late yesterday afternoon. It seems his lordship had been out riding, visiting some tenants, I think Pond said, and on the way home his horse was shot from under him."

"Shot! Who did it?"

The groom shrugged. "No-one was caught. The Earl's groom was too busy seeing what had happened to his master and the horse to pay much attention to anything else, and by the time they'd put the poor animal out of its misery the fellow had gone."

"Might it have been an accident? Poachers, perhaps?" she asked worriedly.

"They were riding alongside a wood. It don't seem likely that a poacher with a gun would be there in broad daylight."

"How do you know so much about it?" Bobby asked, suddenly realising that this had happened less than a day previously.

"Just as I was saddling up Major, Miss Bobby, this groom rode in. His lordship had sent him off with letters — to be delivered first thing this morning. The man had left in the middle of the night, and had taken the letters to the city before coming to Heronforth House."

"Is he there now?"

"Yes, he was told to stay."

Bobby turned her mount and set off towards the Park entrance.

"Come on, Shearer, I must see him."

She hurried back to Berkeley Square and straight to the stables, urged by a vague disquiet she could not define.

"You go and bring the man here, Shearer, but discreetly, pray."

He nodded and disappeared, while Bobby occupied herself with inspecting her carriage horses. After what seemed an eternity Shearer returned with a small wizened man in tow.

"This is Pond, Miss Bobby."

"Let's talk here in the box," Bobby suggested, and heads bent as though they were examining the horses, they spoke in low voices.

"Shearer has told me all he knows, Pond. You were there. Do you think it *could* have been an accident?"

Slowly the groom shook his head. "I've been thinking and puzzling, and nohow could it 'ave been — mind you, it could be made to look like one at need," he replied.

"Why could it not?"

"Poachers 'ave more sense than to take guns on 'is lordship's land. 'Sides, nought but rabbits worth the taking just now, and they'm better trapped wi' wire." He picked up a wisp of hay and sucked it reflectively. "An' there's the place. King's Wood be a fine place to 'ide, but not for shootin'. Too overgrown. Good place to ambush a man though."

"And you think that was what happened?"

He nodded, meeting her eyes firmly. "Aye, that I do, Miss."

"Were you with him the other night, when he was attacked by the highwayman?"

"Yes, Miss Blain, I were, an' I thought that a funny business too."

"Why?"

"I'd wager my last Yellow George that were no reg'lar Toby!"

"What makes you so certain?"

"They don't shoot first. They'm not keen to get the law after 'em, which would be in a killin' matter. Take a few valuables, knock poor devils about, but no killin' 'cept to escape. This cove fired 'is pistol to 'alt us, an' then aimed straight at 'is lordship. 'Twere a mercy that 'e couldn't shoot straight, and that 'is lordship were ready and got 'im instead!"

"When is his lordship returning to London? Did he say?"

"Today or tomorrow, 'e said as 'ow 'e 'ad some matters to deal with, 'an didn't know 'ow long they'd take. I think 'e was goin' to go an' see old Joe Smith," he added meaningly.

"Who is he?"

"Well, Smith used to be Mr Fitzjohn's man, a few years back, about the time the late Lord Heronforth got wed. I don't know the full amount on it, but Mr Fitzjohn turned 'im off, and the late Earl set 'im up in a cottage, wi' a pension, like 'e does for all the old servants past their work."

"Oh, I see. Thank you Pond."

Bobby stood deep in thought, and Pond and Shearer looked at her, waiting for orders. Suddenly she made up her mind.

"Shearer, I'll take the curricle. Harness the horses at once, I cannot wait to change, I will go in my habit."

Shearer and Pond speedily had the

horses and curricle out in the yard, and Shearer sprang up beside his mistress as she took the reins. She drove to George's rooms, and was fortunate to find him in. Leaving Shearer to walk the horses she went in. He had been about to go riding, but at the sight of Bobby he laid down his gloves and whip and welcomed her gaily.

"To what do I owe this pleasure?"

"It is no pleasure," she returned, and then smiled apologetically at his look of surprise. "Oh, pray do not mistake me! I am unable to think properly!"

"What has happened?" he asked in concern. "Here, sit down. Will you take some wine?"

"No, thank you. George, I did not know who else to come to."

"I am honoured you came to me. What in the world has occurred to put you in such a state?"

"I do not know," she replied distractedly. "Oh, I know what has *happened*, but not the meaning of it. I thought, as you are his friend, that you could help me disentangle matters!"

"I am completely in the dark," George

declared. "Who is this 'he'? Heronforth?"

"Of course. It seems too great a coincidence. Did you know that he was shot by a highwayman the night of our party to Vauxhall?"

"What! The devil! How did that happen?"

She explained how she had discovered it, and what Heronforth had told her. Then she repeated what the groom Pond had said about the attack.

"He was certain that it was no ordinary highwayman," she finished.

"It does not sound like it. But how is it that you have been discussing this with Dermot's groom?" he asked in puzzlement.

"Because of what happened yesterday. I was about to tell you, for this is what is so odd. It cannot be chance that he is shot at twice within a few days!"

"Shot at again?" George exclaimed. "How?"

Bobby told him all she had learned from Shearer and directly from Pond.

"This man may be seeing more in it than there is," she said worriedly. "I would have been more certain if it had been different men with him. Pond may exaggerate!"

"I cannot think he does," George said grimly. "Just before you arrived in town Dermot was attacked by some footpads, late one night as he was walking back from Watier's. There were three of them, but he is a handy fellow with the fives, and gave them a trouncing!"

"That makes it more likely that someone is trying to kill him."

It was a bald statement of fact, and they looked at one another in silence. Then George nodded.

"Any one attack could be an accident, on its own. Not three."

"Who is it?"

"Who benefits by his death?"

"Mr Fitzjohn is his heir," Bobby said slowly, voicing the vague suspicions that had been troubling her, "and may be getting desperate if he thinks Heronforth is about to marry."

George shot her a sharp glance, but she was frowning in concentration.

"Did Fitzjohn know where he was these past three days?" George asked.

"Of course! He came to call on Sylvia

the day Dermot — Heronforth left, and she told him all about it. He was behaving oddly that morning, he did not seem to have any real reason for calling, and Sylvia was as surprised to see him as I was."

"Then he would have had time to arrange this. And when the highwayman attacked, Dermot had gone to see to some business at Fitzjohn's house, on the way to St Alban's. He could have known which way and when he planned to return."

"And he was so startled on seeing him at Vauxhall!" Bobby interjected. "Do you remember, he did not even see you!"

"You are right!" George said in excitement. "He must have been surprised to discover that his plans had miscarried! As to the footpads, it's obvious Fitzjohn consorts with some dubious characters; that would have been easy enough to arrange!"

They were silent, well aware that if the Earl were killed Fitzjohn's money problems would be solved. It was the obvious motive for the attempts to murder him. Bobby wondered if these money worries had suddenly become more acute, or whether Mr Fitzjohn had realised that the Earl was more likely to marry Julietta than anyone he had previously met. When he did all possibility of inheriting the title might vanish for Fitzjohn, and the thought could have made him desperate.

"Do you think he knows?" she asked eventually.

"Trust Dermot to be up to snuff," George reassured her. "Of a certainty he will suspect, for he knows full well what kidney Fitzjohn is! Are you afraid he will not be on his guard?"

"He cannot take precautions the whole time, and twice he appears to have escaped only by chance," she said reasonably.

"When does he return to town?"

"Pond was uncertain, but today or tomorrow. I doubt if he will come today, for if he does Sylvia will plague him into attending Lady Staple's masked ball. I do not expect he would wish to, after Vauxhall," she said awkwardly. " I thought that was why he went away, to avoid the ball."

"I would not have thought so. If Dermot wanted to cry off, he would."

"Will you see him tomorrow, and tell him what we suspect?"

"Why cannot you tell him? You live in the same house, after all!"

To his surprise she blushed, and in some confusion shook her head. "I — I cannot! He, oh, he would not believe me, and besides, it would be better coming from a friend! It would seem like meddling on my part!"

"Very well," George said calmly. "I will call on him tomorrow. Now, can I escort you home?"

"No, I thank you. Shearer is with me."

"Then I shall see you tonight?"

"Yes, but you might not discover me under my mask!" she said with attempted lightness.

"I should know your hair anywhere," he said, and she pulled a face at him.

"Hateful colour! If only I were dark! Sylvia thinks I am most unfashionable, and even Aunt Rose bemoans it!"

"Jealousy," he laughed. "It will be of great assistance to me, however, and besides, I like it!"

Bobby laughed, and with a lighter

heart went back to Berkeley Square. She could not help dwelling on the matter, however, and it was mingled with her own problems. If Mr Fitzjohn were capable of murder, could she trust what he had told her earlier? All the rest of that day she pondered the matter, a nagging worry that some vital part of the puzzle was eluding her. By dinner time she had a headache, but had to swallow a draught which Eloise, her maid, obtained from Mrs Chase for her, and descend to help Sylvia entertain Julietta and her brother.

Sylvia was querulous because of Heronforth's continued absence; Julietta was displaying patient suffering; Paul Howe was resentful at being forced away from his masterpiece, and sulky in consequence; Aunt Rose attempted to keep the conversation going, but merely succeeded in irritating everyone present. Bobby hoped that the ball would make up for this inauspicious beginning. She replied automatically to her aunt's comments, and then, when Sylvia joined in the conversation, retired into her own thoughts.

Suddenly she realised that Sylvia was

reminiscing about her own wedding, and slyly hinting that Julietta would soon be preparing for her own. The thought that had been eluding her all day was, startlingly, in the forefront of her mind. Surely, when Sylvia had been complaining about Mr Fitzjohn she had intimated that she had not met Dermot until after her wedding. In which case, if the party Mr Fitzjohn had told her about had taken place just before, this was impossible. Had Fitzjohn been lying to her? Or, and her leaping heart missed a beat at the thought, was Sylvia, often vague, incorrect in what she had said?

Impatiently Bobby waited for the dinner to finish. Mr Fitzjohn would be at the ball. She was determined to face him with her suspicions. At the sudden animated look on her face, Sylvia broke off what she was saying and enquired solicitously if she were well.

Bobby smiled at her. "Oh yes, I am simply looking forward to the ball!" she replied.

"Well, I am not, unless I can change my slippers," Julietta said pettishly. "Paul, you will have to take me home to change them, they are pinching my toes! That wretched maid has not stretched them properly!"

Sylvia was all sympathy. "Poor dear! The carriage shall drop Bobby and me at Lady Staple's and then take you home, so that you will be comfortable."

"I think I shall change my gown too," Julietta said consideringly.

Bobby grinned. Julietta had worn the new gown, but obviously considered that it would be wasteful to hide it under a domino.

At last they were ready. Bobby bade Aunt Rose goodnight, and they set off. When she arrived at Lady Staple's house, she went immediately to seek out Mr Fitzjohn. There were not a great number of people present so early, and she soon found him, recognising him by his patchy grey hair, as he in turn recognised her by her red-gold curls.

"I must speak with you," she said quietly, and he smiled agreement.

"You look charmingly," he murmured as he led her to a secluded alcove.

"You remember our conversation about

my father," she said, ignoring his compliments, "when you told me of that game. When did it take place? Was it before James' wedding?"

"But yes," he said in surprise. "I thought I had said so."

"I wished to make sure, because I have now heard that Der — the Earl, was not in England then, and did not meet Sylvia until after her wedding!"

"Who told you this? Sylvia herself?"

"Yes."

He shrugged and laughed. "Really, my dear! Have you not yet discovered what a shatter-brained female my cousin is? Of course he was here. Not for long, I grant, but he was most decidedly there, at that game. Have you been disbelieving me?"

"Who can I believe?" she retorted. "What proof is there apart from your story, and Sylvia's assertion that she did not meet her brother-in-law until after the wedding? How can it be proved?"

He looked at her consideringly. "I am hurt, deeply, by the distrust you obviously have for me! Naturally I would not have invented a story so discreditable to Dermot! I have proof. You know the

Earl's signature, I suppose?"

Bobby nodded, recalling the letter that had come from him before she had come to London, and the franking he had often given her letters.

"Then I have a document, a signed confession, that James left in my care. He made Dermot sign it, for he feared that at some future time a similar thing might happen. It was a safeguard against that, and given to me for me to use as a threat. James knew that this would be sufficient to keep Dermot from such tricks again."

Bobby stared at him, her wild hopes of the last hour collapsing about her.

"I must see it," she said in a low voice, clinging to the hope that it was a bluff.

"When? I have it in my rooms. Shall we slip away from here and take a hackney now? No-one will miss us for a half hour, and my rooms are only a few minutes away?"

All thought of caution for her reputation was abandoned, and numbly she nodded agreement. She had to know, and this would finally prove it. As if in a daze she allowed Mr Fitzjohn to guide her out of the house and a little way along the street to where he hailed a hackney. He helped her inside, and she sat in silent misery for the few minutes it took to drive to North Audley Street. Too distressed to care for what she was doing she went into the house and up to his rooms, turning to face him as he shut the door of his sitting room.

"Is it true?" she asked despairingly.

"I wish I could say it were not, if you care so much, my dear," he answered. "Here, it has all been rather a shock. I will get you some brandy."

He went across to a table and poured the brandy out. She sank into a chair and looked sightlessly at the flowers in the bowl set in the otherwise empty fireplace. He brought the goblet to her, and laid a hand gently on her shoulder.

"Drink this, my dear."

She meekly obeyed, and the fiery spirit revived her slightly.

"Where is this — confession?" she asked dully.

"In a safe place in my bedroom. I will fetch it, but meanwhile I will fill your glass."

He did so, and she did not object. He disappeared into the adjoining room, and Bobby slowly sipped the brandy. Her headache was far worse now, the healing effect of Mrs Chase's draught having worn off, she supposed, and she felt rather faint. This was a novel sensation to Bobby, who had never swooned in her life, and she rested her head against the back of the chair, closing her eyes.

Some time later she reopened them to find Mr Fitzjohn standing beside her. She tried to rise, but found that her limbs would not obey her.

"Where is the confession?" she asked, but to her ears the words were slurred.

He handed her a sheet of paper, and with an effort she tried to fix her gaze on it.

"I cannot see any writing," she said after a while.

Mr Fitzjohn laughed. "There is none," he told her in a triumphant voice.

"Then, why? What have you done? Oh, the brandy! You put something in it!"

She tried to rise, but the drug had taken speedy effect, and she could scarcely move. She could still speak, however.

"You are trying to murder me too!" she whispered.

He raised his eyebrows. "So you had guessed that? No, my dear, I do not intend murder, for either of you! I have a neater plan. I would like to become Earl, true, but a fortune would suit me just as well, especially, my dear Bobby, with you also!"

Her senses were gradually slipping away from her. "What do you mean?" she gasped.

"I cannot allow my dear cousin to marry you, and deprive me of both title and fortune!" he replied. "I shall marry you instead, and then you will not be able to betray me. Do not fear, we shall deal together well."

With a last effort, she attempted to explain that Heronforth did not wish to marry her, but by now her words were slurred, and he did not catch them.

"How did I know? Sylvia gave a broad enough hint when I called on her. But it shall not be. Tomorrow I shall take you into the country, and arrange a marriage. You will have no alternative, you know," he added as she weakly shook her head, "after spending the night here in my rooms."

Fighting against the knowledge, Bobby again attempted to rise, but to no avail, and her last conscious sensation was of falling, sliding down from the chair, Fitzjohn's arm thrown out to catch her as she sank into deep oblivion.

11

THE Earl of Heronforth entered his breakfast parlour at his usual hour, to find taking place there a scene unprecedented in his normally well conducted household. A young woman he recognised as Eloise, the French maid Bobby had engaged, was being forcibly pushed towards the door by his staid butler, while footmen goggled helplessly in the background.

"What goes on?" he demanded in a voice which brought them all to a sudden horrified realisation of the enormity of their offence, and caused Eloise to cease for a moment her excited lamentations.

Shenstone recovered himself first.

"I was informing Miss Blain's maid that you would no doubt be willing to see her and listen to what she has to say *after* you have eaten, my lord," he said repressively.

"It cannot wait, you *imbecile!*" Eloise almost wept, and, free of his restraining hands, flung herself on the Earl, grasping, in her extreme agitation, the lapels of his coat.

"Be calm, and tell me at once," he commanded, and recognising his air of authority she allowed him to put her into the chair the disapproving Shenstone pulled out for her.

"When I go to my mistress's room this morning, she is not there! She is gone, and her bed, it is not slept in!" the girl sobbed.

"Why didn't you say so at once, you jobberknowl!" Shenstone cried, for he was very fond of Miss Blain, and this distressing news made him forget his years of training and discipline.

"You would not permit it!" Eloise flashed back at him.

"Be silent, the pair of you. Now, who was on the door last night when her ladyship returned from the ball?"

One of the footmen edged forward. "I was, me lord."

"At what time did Miss Blain return from the ball, or did she not?"

The man gulped. "Well, it were like this, me lord. 'Er ladyship came in soon after midnight, and there were a proper commotion, for she were moanin' fit to — she were ill," he substituted. "I 'elped carry 'er up to 'er room, and then I were sent 'ot foot to fetch 'er maid who went in to 'er. I thought Miss Blain must 'ave come in then, for there were such a bustle I never knew if I were on me 'ead or me 'eels."

Heronforth nodded. "And she did not come in later?"

The man shook his head. His lordship turned to Eloise.

"You did not wait up for Miss Blain?"

"She will not allow it, my lord, though I would prefer to, and wish that I had!"

He smiled comfortingly. "It is none of your fault. Come with me now to her ladyship's room."

He swept her up the stairs, leaving the unfortunate footman to bear the full brunt of Shenstone's displeasure, both on account of his incompetence and laziness in not knowing who was returned and who not, and his inability to express himself in a seemly manner in the presence of his betters.

The Earl knocked imperiously on Sylvia's bedroom door, and then told Eloise to go in and inform her ladyship that he wished to see her immediately. Complaining tones reached him from inside the room, and a subdued Eloise appeared at the door to inform him that her ladyship refused.

"I must see you and I am coming in, Sylvia," the Earl announced, and walked into the room to find an indignant Sylvia staring at him furiously.

"Dermot! Have you run mad? This is the outside of enough! Leave my room immediately, and take this impertinent chit with you!"

"When you have told me what I wish to know," he replied urbanely. "At what time did you return last night, and did Bobby come with you?'

Frightened suddenly by his air of implacability, Sylvia forgot to seek refuge in her usual tears and tantrums.

"I felt unwell, and came home about midnight," she gasped. "Why? What in the world has happened?"

"Bobby has not come home. Was she with you?"

"No! I could not find her, in all the masks!"

"So you left her there alone, unchaperoned?" he thundered.

She cowered back amongst the pillows.

"Of course not! Do you think me lost to all sense of propriety? She is a friend of Lady Staple, and I arranged for Julietta and her brother to escort Bobby home at the end of the ball! It is all your fault for arriving home so late that you could not escort us to the ball," she added, recovering slightly. "No doubt she has run off in a huff after her cousin's rejection!"

"What do you mean?" he demanded.

"Mr Holt is betrothed to little Celia Sawley," she reported maliciously. "Bobby was not pleased, as you can imagine!"

"She is not so poor spirited, but you have betrayed your trust as her hostess, and your position as James' widow!" he said coldly, and strode out of the room, followed by Eloise, and leaving a distracted Sylvia crying after him to be told what it was all about. Ignoring her he went to Bobby's room and looked inside.

"Has she taken anything?" he asked Eloise, and the girl shook her head.

"I look for her jewels, but they are all there, except the pearls she wore last night and the ruby ring. And I am certain, *absolument*, that nothing else is taken. She was *not* distressed, she did not wish in the least to marry this cousin," Eloise added in defence of her mistress.

He smiled at her briefly, encouragingly.

"Remain here and do your best to calm Miss Holt when she hears of it," he ordered. "I have no doubt that I shall soon discover her."

He ran down the stairs to find Shenstone waiting for instructions in the hall.

"Have my curricle sent round to Miss Howe's, with the fastest horses," he ordered. "I shall walk there to save time, it is only a few minutes, but I may need to go further. Tell her ladyship that my orders are that she breathes no word of this to anyone else, on pain of my deepest displeasure!"

Despite his worry, Shenstone could not forbear a faint smile at the thought of this task, and helped his master into the many-caped greatcoat he wore for driving. Then the Earl set off, walking rapidly across the Square.

At Julietta's he had to wait, fuming impotently, while Mrs Howe was fetched to deal with this unusual situation, and then had to explain to her that it was imperative that he had immediate speech with her daughter. She regarded his unloverlike countenance with some disquiet, but was at last persuaded to send for Julietta, who appeared after a considerable interval, charmingly attired, but looking rather wary.

"I understand from Sylvia that you were to escort Bobby home last night," he began brusquely. Julietta had never before heard him use that tone of voice.

"I was going to, indeed," she responded, "but at the end of the ball she could not be found. I assumed that she must have found some other escort, having discovered that Sylvia had gone."

"Who might that have been?" he asked sharply.

"Mr Fitzjohn, I suppose," she said with a shrug.

"Why should you think that?"

"Well, I saw her going off with him when we arrived," Julietta said innocently, glancing up at him under her long lashes.

"Were you not all masked? How could you know them?"

"Yes, but I recognised her hair as she stepped into the hackney, and Mr Fitzjohn had taken off his mask."

"Did you not attend the ball together? I understood that you were dining with Sylvia?"

"We did, but my shoes were pinching abominably, and Paul brought me home after dinner to change them. I could not find the ones I wanted, since my stupid maid had taken them off to do something with them, so I had to wear another pair, and also change my gown, so we arrived about half an hour after Sylvia and Bobby. But what in the world has happened to put you in such a passion?"

He did not answer the question. "Are you certain it was Fitzjohn?"

"Yes, of course. Has Bobby eloped with him?" she asked eagerly. "She must have been desperate!"

He had gone, however, without his

usual courtesy, and she was left alone to speculate with satisfaction on what Bobby had done and how she could turn this development to her own advantage.

The Earl found the groom Pond waiting outside with the curricle. The man was agog with curiosity, but the Earl merely nodded his thanks and sprang in, turning towards North Audley Street. As he reached the house where his cousin lodged he leaped out, flung the reins to Pond, and ran up the steps. He plied the knocker vigorously and swore at the delay until the old man who owned the house appeared.

"I must have speech with Mr Fitzjohn at once," the Earl stated, displaying a coin.

The man eyed it regretfully. "I'm afeard that's impossible, my lord, for your cousin left town an hour ago."

The Earl breathed a sigh of relief. He had feared that it would have been the previous night.

"Alone? Do you know where he went?"

"He had a wench with him. She seemed half daft," the man mused.

"Where did they go?"

"I'm not too sure, but he headed northwards."

"My thanks." The Earl handed the man the coin. "Now it is not that I disbelieve you, but that cousin of mine is a slippery fellow. I must look round his rooms."

The man opened the door wide and led the Earl up to Mr Fitzjohn's rooms, which were obviously empty. He looked around, and pounced on a mask that lay discarded on the floor. It was edged with fine lace, and was too small to be his cousin's own. On looking closely he saw a couple of red-gold hairs caught in the ribbon, and his fists clenched as he stared at them. Abruptly he turned and ran down the stairs into the street. As he strode across to his curricle he was hailed from across the street.

"Dermot, wait!"

It was George, on horseback, and looking anxious.

"Is she here?" he demanded, and the Earl shook his head.

"Why did you think she would be?" he demanded swiftly.

"If you know where she is, let me come with you and explain on the way,"

George suggested, and at the Earl's nod, he dismounted, gave his horse to Pond with instructions to return it to its stable, and swung himself up into the curricle after the Earl.

"He's gone northwards, which probably means he is making for his house beyond Barnet," Heronforth said tersely.

"Let's pray we are in time."

"They've only an hour's start. But how do you come to be here?"

"I went to see you, and Shenstone told me. He said you would not object to my knowing. She came to me yesterday, having heard of the latest attack on you, and we were both convinced Fitzjohn had something to do with it. She was frantic with worry, and I'll wager that she thought to do some idiotic thing last night. I wish I had realised when I failed to discover her at the ball, but I arrived late, and as neither she nor Sylvia were there, thought they had gone early. This morning I went to you, and hearing what had happened, came straight round here."

Heronforth related the story as he had pieced it together, and they then relapsed into silence, the Earl concentrating on getting every ounce of speed out of his horses once they left London behind. He nursed them carefully on the long pull up Highgate Hill, and then, the road being freer of traffic, he urged them on. They passed through Barnet without seeing the other curricle, but a mile or so out of the town Heronforth suddenly pointed with his whip. They had just rounded a slight bend in the road, and there in front of them, some distance away, was another curricle containing two persons.

"We'll not overtake them too quickly," the Earl said as George urged him to spring the horses. "That might alarm him, and my pair have not much left in them for a chase. I want to come up as close as I can before he is aware of it."

He increased his speed gradually, and they drew nearer the vehicle in front, until they could see Bobby's bright curls and recognise Fitzjohn. The distance between the two curricles had narrowed to a hundred yards or so when Mr Fitzjohn glanced back over his shoulder. He took another look, and then urged his horses to a gallop. Immediately the Earl pushed on his own, and they raced along, the gap inexorably lessening.

Earlier that morning Bobby had awoken, her head feeling like a heavy lump of lead, her mouth having in it a foul taste, and her senses so disordered that it had taken her some time to realise that she was still attired in her ball gown, and had been sleeping in a chair. It was some minutes later before she was able to recall the events that had led up to that moment when she had realised that Mr Fitzjohn had tricked her, and had rendered her powerless by administering some drug in the brandy he had given her.

She looked about her as her memory returned, and found that she was still in Mr Fitzjohn's sitting room. He was nowhere to be seen, and she felt a faint hope that she might be able to escape from his rooms. It was already daylight, and quite late in the morning, she judged, for the curtains had not been drawn and the sunlight poured into the room. Cautiously she moved her limbs, and then discovered that her ankles had been secured by thin cords, and were tied to the legs of the chair. As she tried to stretch out her hands to untie them, she was brought up short, and found that they too had been tied, each to the arm of the chair, and so that she could not put them together.

No wonder he had been able to leave her, and was himself no doubt taking his ease in a comfortable bed, she thought angrily. The surge of fury made her head ache again, and she groaned, unable to move far to ease her position. The sound was heard; possibly Mr Fitzjohn had been listening for it, for almost at once the door leading to his bedroom opened and he appeared. He was dressed immaculately, a fresh cravat about his neck, and Bobby ground her teeth together as she compared his state with her own crumpled disorder.

"I hope you did not pass too uncomfortable a night, my dear," he said as he came towards her. "Shall I loosen your bonds? Will you be sensible and not resist?"

Bobby did not reply, but he obviously thought her incapable of resisting, for he swiftly cut the cords that had imprisoned her. She weakly stretched out her arms, and found to her dismay that she could barely move.

"You will feel better after you have washed and had something to eat," he told her. "My man has brought up some more hot water, and you may use my room to freshen yourself up. Do not think to escape that way, however, the other door is locked."

He came across to help her to her feet, but she angrily waved him away, and with a tremendous effort forced herself to rise, and to cross the endless few yards to the door he held for her. Once inside she almost collapsed onto the bed, but deep inside herself knew that the only way she could help herself was to restore her wits as quickly as possible. She found a jug of cold water, and spurning the steaming water in the bowl, splashed the cold water over her face, gasping at the shock, but immediately feeling better.

Shivering with distaste, she used the comb she found and dragged her curls into some sort of order, and then, feeling much stronger, returned to the sitting room.

A tray with a pot of chocolate and

some slices of thin bread and butter had been brought in, and was placed on a small table beside the chair. Mr Fitzjohn was seated at another table, busy with a plate piled high with slices of beef, and a tankard of ale. He waved her to the chair.

"Help yourself, my dear. After we have broken our fast we are driving out to my house beyond Barnet."

She walked across to the chair as if in a daze, unwilling to let him know that she was already feeling so much better. Suspicious of the chocolate, she poured herself half a cup, but did not drink it. She doubted in any case whether she could have done so, but she was able to nibble at the bread and butter, and this helped to restore her.

When Mr Fitzjohn had finished, he came and stood beside her.

"I am driving you out to my house, and after we have eaten there, and I have made certain arrangements, we will be on our way to Scotland. I feel sure that, once you have accepted the inevitability of this, my dear, you will be sensible and make the best of life as my wife. I am aware that you are not in favour of it yet, and so I must tie your hands together. We cannot afford any — er — accidents, while I am driving."

She did not appear to have heard him, and he bent down, grasping her hands which lay limp in her lap, and bound them together with more of the thin cord he had used before. Then he pulled her to her feet and fastened her cloak about her shoulders, so that it hid her hands. She knew the futility of resisting, and had to hope that her appearance of being still half drugged would disarm his suspicions, and allow her to make a bid for freedom later on, when she felt stronger.

He had almost to carry her down the stairs, and out to where his curricle was waiting. Picking her up he lifted her into the vehicle, and then tucked a rug about her knees, before nodding dismissal to his own groom who had held the horses, and driving off. This was a disappointment to Bobby, who had hoped that she might be able to beg assistance from the man, but she took comfort in the fact that the fresh air was fast reviving her.

Mr Fitzjohn made occasional comments

to her as they drove steadily out of London. He did not appear to be in a hurry, but as Bobby could not imagine how anyone might have discovered her whereabouts and be following them, there was not much joy in that. She did not bother to answer him, sitting with her eyes half closed as though she were still in a daze. She had soon discovered that the knots which he had made to secure her hands were loose, and by patiently working on them under cover of the rug she was at last able to free her hands.

When they reached Barnet she was hopeful that they would stop to change horses, and that she would be able to cry for help from other travellers, but he drove straight through, telling her that his house was not far beyond.

"We will drive into St Albans later today, and then travel post northwards," he said, smiling. "It will appear a most romantic affair."

"I shall not marry you," she said in a low voice.

"Your reputation, after staying the night in my rooms, is utterly ruined, my dear. You have no alternative."

"I do not need to marry you," she insisted, not allowing her voice to show much strength.

"There are ways to force you," he replied, and despite herself, Bobby shivered.

He glanced down at her, a cruel look on his face, and then looked over his shoulder.

"The devil!" He turned round further to look again, and Bobby looked to see what had distracted him. To her astonishment she saw, some way behind them, another curricle with the Earl of Heronforth driving, and George sitting beside him. For a moment she thought that the drug must still be having odd effects, and that she was dreaming, but when Mr Fitzjohn lashed up his horses, driving them into a headlong gallop, she knew that help really was at hand.

The pursuing curricle drew nearer, gradually overhauling them, and Mr Fitzjohn swore lustily at his horses. Then he dragged from his pocket a pistol, and turned to take aim at his cousin, who was now only a few horses' lengths behind. Bobby flung herself sideways and pushed his arm upwards as the pistol exploded, and then attempted to grab the reins from him. She was still, however, very weak, and he easily held her off, cursing her, Dermot, and his horses indiscriminately. She saw that he had another pistol which he was attempting to get out of his pocket, and she clung desperately to his arm, hampering him and preventing him from freeing it from the clinging folds of his coat.

The struggle had made it impossible for Fitzjohn to drive, and the horses, terrified by the report of the pistol, were now bolting madly along the road, the curricle swaying wildly from side to side. The horses failed to take a slight bend in the road, the near wheel of the curricle tipped into the ditch, and the last thing Bobby remembered was being flung out of the vehicle as it overturned.

The Earl of Heronforth, from the moment he had realised that Mr Fitzjohn was armed and prepared to use his pistols, had been concentrating on getting the fastest possible pace out of his by now exceedingly tired horses. Watching the struggle ahead of him, his lips pressed tightly together, and his eyes narrowed to a fierce slit, he thought that he would be capable of murder if his wretched cousin harmed Bobby. He realised a moment before it happened that the other curricle was going to come to grief, and hauled his own pair to a standstill.

Leaping down from his seat, ignoring the still body of his cousin as it lay in the road, he ran to where Bobby had fallen, and George, who had been sympathetically aware of his emotions during that wild chase, went to release the frantic horses, trapped by the ruined curricle.

Bobby opened her eyes a few moments later to find the Earl kneeling beside her, one arm about her shoulders as he supported her, the other hand gently feeling her head for bruises. She struggled to sit up.

"Stay still," he ordered firmly, "until you are feeling more the thing."

She laughed weakly. "I am not ill! Truly I feel better!"

"Which is why you passed out, I presume," he retorted. "Does your head hurt? You fell into a bush, so your fall was broken, but you must have hit your head on something."

"I expect it was the sudden movement, after the drug," she replied, feeling remarkably clear headed and safe now that he was there. "What of — him?"

"We'll see to him in a moment," he assured her, glancing to where his cousin lay a few feet away.

"No need," George said, coming up to them. "Are you in one piece, Bobby?"

She smiled and nodded. "How did you know? How did you come to follow us?"

"We'll leave the explanations for later," Heronforth said. "Now we'd better look to Percy."

"There is no need," George repeated. "He must have had another pistol in his pocket, and it fired when the curricle overturned. He's dead."

The Earl glanced swiftly across at his cousin's body, then at Bobby. She was gazing in dismay at Mr Fitzjohn, but the news did not appear to upset her unduly. He looked back at George.

"His house is but a few miles from here. If I take Bobby directly there in my curricle, can you go to the nearest farm and arrange for a cart to bring his body?"

"Of course. Take Bobby away from here."

Before Bobby was really aware of what was happening she found herself being lifted in the Earl's strong arms and carried to his curricle, where he wrapped a rug about her, and then sprang up beside her and drove off, waving to George left to deal with the consequences of the accident. When she began an attempt to explain how she had come to be in such a situation, he shook his head and smiled down at her.

"Not now. I will have Percy's housekeeper put you to bed, and then, when you have had time to recover, you shall tell it me."

Realising that she was exceedingly tired, she thankfully lapsed into silence, and was half asleep when they halted outside a pleasant manor house. Heronforth lifted her down, and in response to her protests, allowed her to walk up the steps to the front door. She did not listen to the explanation he gave to the servants who admitted them, but soon found herself whisked upstairs, helped by a motherly woman who undressed her and put her into a huge, soft bed.

It was almost dark when she awoke, and for some minutes she could not recall how she came to be in this strange room. Then it all returned to her, and she sat up, relieved to find that she was feeling her normal self. She dressed quickly, and then made her way out onto the landing and down the stairs. At the foot she hesitated, but the Earl appeared from a room to her right, and smilingly held open the door for her.

"Are you better? Then we will have dinner. Come in here until it is ready."

He held out his hand, and rather shyly she took it and allowed him to lead her into a brightly furnished parlour, gay with bowls of flowers. She looked round, expecting to see George, but he was not there.

"Where is George?" she asked.

"Do not be afraid that he has left you to my tender mercies," he answered with a laugh. "He has just gone to make himself tidy for dinner. Now, do you feel strong enough to tell me what happened?"

Haltingly, Bobby began by explaining how her father had been accused of cheating at cards, and how she had determined to clear his name, and how she had learned from Mr Fitzjohn after her game of piquet that her father had not been guilty. At this point, still unsure of the Earl's own guilt, she faltered to a stop.

"Whom did he accuse?" Heronforth asked, a trifle grimly, she thought.

"He said it was you," she replied in a low voice. "I — I did not know what to believe, but his story could have been true." She repeated the version she had heard from Mr Fitzjohn. "Then something Sylvia said made me think you could not have been in England at that time, and I challenged him with it. He said he had a signed confession, and I went with him to see. Oh, I was a fool! I should have realised he had some trick, especially when I suspected him of trying to kill you! But I was dazed, distraught to think that you — I — I could not believe it, whatever he said," she finished lamely.

"What happened then?" he asked

evenly, and she told him how she had been drugged, and then forced to accompany Fitzjohn.

"He said he would marry me and my fortune, instead of trying to obtain yours, so that was a confession. Did you know he had attacked you?" she asked eagerly.

"Yes, I was almost sure, but I had another matter to deal with. The version he gave you of the card game, and your father's part in it was almost correct. I was not there, as you suspected, and it was James who cheated. From then until his death Percy had been milking James of a small fortune. I began to suspect something of the sort soon after I inherited, and then I found a paper that gave me a clue Percy was involved. I have been trying to fit the pieces of the puzzle together for some months, and had almost enough evidence to force Percy out of the country, by threatening to expose him if he did not go. He was desperate for money since James' death, and hoped to inherit by killing me. This need became more urgent once I seemed about to marry."

Bobby had been smiling at him with

immense relief since he had explained that it was his brother and not he that had cheated, but on his last words she dropped her eyes quickly. He gave a low laugh and walked across the room to stand before her where she sat.

"Now you can clear your father's name," he said softly.

"What is the purpose of reviving an old scandal?" she answered quietly. "They are all dead now, and I am content to know the truth. Oh, if they had still been alive, I would have wanted vengeance, but as it is, I can return home satisfied."

"Are you disenchanted with town life?" he asked.

"No, but — this affair will be noised abroad, and it will cause less talk if I go home."

"No-one knows who cannot be induced to remain quiet about it. I cannot allow such talk about the Countess of Heronforth," he said softly.

"Sylvia? What has she to do with it?" she asked, puzzled.

He laughed, and she found that he had captured her hands and was pulling her to her feet, and then his arms were about her and he was drawing her close to him.

"Darling idiot!" he admonished. "Sylvia is the dowager Countess."

She giggled at the thought, but stared up at him, wondering if she had heard aright, or whether the drug was still having some odd effect on her.

"I need a Countess of my own, to protect me from all those husband-hunting females," he told her teasingly, "and you most decidedly need a husband to keep you from falling into the most abominable scrapes! Oh, Bobby, my love, little did I guess when I thought my peace would be broken for a short while by having to bear-lead a stripling about the town that it was going to be permanently broken because I would fall in love with you! The only possible way you can restore me some peace will be to say you will marry me!"

"Why me?" was all she could think of in response to this.

He grinned down at her. "So you want compliments as well? Do you need to be told that you are the most lovely, delightful, exasperating female it has been my misfortune to encounter? That I never have a moment's peace when I am away from you, wondering what mischief you will be getting into next? That you have the most tantalising smile and lips that I shall never tire of kissing? Like this?" he finished, demonstrating in no uncertain manner what he meant.

Bobby felt herself weak with the ecstasy of it, and realised that here was what she had sought and not found in Jeremy, a mutual love that had not been possible with George, a love such as she had never expected to find, offered her by this man who was crushing her in his arms and making her breathless with his kisses. At last he lifted his mouth from hers and stood, holding her tightly still, his eyes only a few inches from hers.

"Well? Will you marry me, my adorable one? Will you put me out of the misery I have been in since I first thought you betrothed to Jeremy?"

"I never was," she said indignantly.

He laughed. "No, but enough people contrived to make me aware that you might be," he retorted. "If I had been aware of his existence, and the risk that I might have lost you, I would have proposed to you the first night I saw you, for I knew then that you were the girl for me! Well, what of my question? Do you come willingly, or must I carry you to Scotland by force? Or shall I simply compromise you by keeping you here? It is in any event too late to drive back to London tonight."

"Oh, Aunt Rose! She will be frantic!" Bobby exclaimed.

"Not so, for I dispatched a groom to tell them all was well," he reassured her. "Now, do I have to send George away too, or shall he stay to play propriety, if you accept my offer?"

She laughed shakily. "I must be dreaming! Oh, Dermot! Tell me I am not!"

He did so in the only possible manner, and when he again released her he looked deep into her eyes.

"Stop prevaricating, my love. When will you marry me? My house is waiting, you have ample clothes, and we will choose more for you in Paris. All you have to do is order a wedding gown and choose some of the jewels I mean to buy for you. Aunt Rose and Sylvia will be in their element organising a reception and all the rest of it, and the sooner it is all done and you are mine the better. When shall it be?"

She smiled at him, shyly. "Whenever you wish, Dermot."

He folded her into a close embrace which ended only when George walked into the room to announce that dinner was about to be served. Dermot turned towards him, while Bobby blushed at being discovered clasped in the Earl's arms.

"Wish us happy, George," he said simply, and George, after a swift look at Bobby's glowing face, shook his hand warmly.

"You have the luck of the devil," he commented. "If he does not treat you properly, Bobby, you have only to call on me and I will roast him alive!"

"She is going to obey me in every single thing," the Earl said, laughing. "That is the only way I can have peace!"

"In the first place I doubt if that will last beyond the honeymoon," George retorted, "and in the second, if she did you would be bored! Well, Bobby, I'm lucky at cards. Will you play me at piquet one day?"

Bobby laughed, her embarrassment gone at George's philosophical reception of the news. She glanced demurely at the Earl.

"Since Dermot has forbidden me to play in public, I shall have to make other arrangements," she said innocently, and then laughed at the expression on the Earl's face.

"Certainly, but I shall have to be there to see fair play," he retorted swiftly, "and *after* our honeymoon!"

Other titles in the
Ulverscroft Large Print Series:

TO FIGHT THE WILD
Rod Ansell and Rachel Percy

Lost in uncharted Australian bush, Rod Ansell survived by hunting and trapping wild animals, improvising shelter and using all the bushman's skills he knew.

COROMANDEL
Pat Barr

India in the 1830s is a hot, uncomfortable place, where the East India Company still rules. Amelia and her new husband find themselves caught up in the animosities which seethe between the old order and the new.

THE SMALL PARTY
Lillian Beckwith

A frightening journey to safety begins for Ruth and her small party as their island is caught up in the dangers of armed insurrection.

THE WILDERNESS WALK
Sheila Bishop

Stifling unpleasant memories of a misbegotten romance in Cleave with Lord Francis Aubrey, Lavinia goes on holiday there with her sister. The two women are thrust into a romantic intrigue involving none other than Lord Francis.

THE RELUCTANT GUEST
Rosalind Brett

Ann Calvert went to spend a month on a South African farm with Theo Borland and his sister. They both proved to be different from her first idea of them, and there was Storr Peterson — the most disturbing man she had ever met.

ONE ENCHANTED SUMMER
Anne Tedlock Brooks

A tale of mystery and romance and a girl who found both during one enchanted summer.

CLOUD OVER MALVERTON
Nancy Buckingham

Dulcie soon realises that something is seriously wrong at Malverton, and when violence strikes she is horrified to find herself under suspicion of murder.

AFTER THOUGHTS
Max Bygraves

The Cockney entertainer tells stories of his East End childhood, of his RAF days, and his post-war showbusiness successes and friendships with fellow comedians.

MOONLIGHT AND MARCH ROSES
D. Y. Cameron

Lynn's search to trace a missing girl takes her to Spain, where she meets Clive Hendon. While untangling the situation, she untangles her emotions and decides on her own future.

NURSE ALICE IN LOVE
Theresa Charles

Accepting the post of nurse to little Fernie Sherrod, Alice Everton could not guess at the romance, suspense and danger which lay ahead at the Sherrod's isolated estate.

POIROT INVESTIGATES
Agatha Christie

Two things bind these eleven stories together — the brilliance and uncanny skill of the diminutive Belgian detective, and the stupidity of his Watson-like partner, Captain Hastings.

LET LOOSE THE TIGERS
Josephine Cox

Queenie promised to find the long-lost son of the frail, elderly murderess, Hannah Jason. But her enquiries threatened to unlock the cage where crucial secrets had long been held captive.

THE TWILIGHT MAN
Frank Gruber

Jim Rand lives alone in the California desert awaiting death. Into his hermit existence comes a teenage girl who blows both his past and his brief future wide open.

DOG IN THE DARK
Gerald Hammond

Jim Cunningham breeds and trains gun dogs, and his antagonism towards the devotees of show spaniels earns him many enemies. So when one of them is found murdered, the police are on his doorstep within hours.

THE RED KNIGHT
Geoffrey Moxon

When he finds himself a pawn on the chessboard of international espionage with his family in constant danger, Guy Trent becomes embroiled in moves and countermoves which may mean life or death for Western scientists.

TIGER TIGER
Frank Ryan

A young man involved in drugs is found murdered. This is the first event which will draw Detective Inspector Sandy Woodings into a whirlpool of murder and deceit.

CAROLINE MINUSCULE
Andrew Taylor

Caroline Minuscule, a medieval script, is the first clue to the whereabouts of a cache of diamonds. The search becomes a deadly kind of fairy story in which several murders have an other-worldly quality.

LONG CHAIN OF DEATH
Sarah Wolf

During the Second World War four American teenagers from the same town join the Army together. Forty-two years later, the son of one of the soldiers realises that someone is systematically wiping out the families of the four men.

THE LISTERDALE MYSTERY
Agatha Christie

Twelve short stories ranging from the light-hearted to the macabre, diverse mysteries ingeniously and plausibly contrived and convincingly unravelled.

TO BE LOVED
Lynne Collins

Andrew married the woman he had always loved despite the knowledge that Sarah married him for reasons of her own. So much heartache could have been avoided if only he had known how vital it was to be loved.

ACCUSED NURSE
Jane Converse

Paula found herself accused of a crime which could cost her her job, her nurse's reputation, and even the man she loved, unless the truth came to light.

BUTTERFLY MONTANE
Dorothy Cork

Parma had come to New Guinea to marry Alec Rivers, but she found him completely disinterested and that overbearing Pierce Adams getting entirely the wrong idea about her.

HONOURABLE FRIENDS
Janet Daley

Priscilla Burford is happily married when she meets Junior Environment Minister Alistair Thurston. Inevitably, sexual obsession and political necessity collide.

WANDERING MINSTRELS
Mary Delorme

Stella Wade's career as a concert pianist might have been ruined by the rudeness of a famous conductor, so it seemed to her agent and benefactor. Even Sir Nicholas fails to see the possibilities when John Tallis falls deeply in love with Stella.

MORNING IS BREAKING
Lesley Denny

The growing frenzy of war catapults Diane Clements into a clandestine marriage and separation with a German refugee.

LAST BUS TO WOODSTOCK
Colin Dexter

A girl's body is discovered huddled in the courtyard of a Woodstock pub, and Detective Chief Inspector Morse and Sergeant Lewis are hunting a rapist and a murderer.

THE STUBBORN TIDE
Anne Durham

Everyone advised Carol not to grieve so excessively over her cousin's death. She might have followed their advice if the man she loved thought that way about her, but another girl came first in his affections.

FATAL RING OF LIGHT
Helen Eastwood

Katy's brother was supposed to have died in 1897 but a scrawled note in his handwriting showed July 1899. What had happened to him in those two years? Katy was determined to help him.

NIGHT ACTION
Alan Evans

Captain David Brent sails at dead of night to the German occupied Normandy town of St. Jean on a mission which will stretch loyalty and ingenuity to its limits, and beyond.

A MURDER TOO MANY
Elizabeth Ferrars

Many, including the murdered man's widow, believed the wrong man had been convicted. The further murder of a key witness in the earlier case convinced Basnett that the seemingly unrelated deaths were linked.

A GREAT DELIVERANCE
Elizabeth George

Into the web of old houses and secrets of Keldale Valley comes Scotland Yard Inspector Thomas Lynley and his assistant to solve a particularly savage murder.

'E' IS FOR EVIDENCE
Sue Grafton

Kinsey Millhone was bogged down on a warehouse fire claim. It came as something of a shock when she was accused of being on the take. She'd been set up. Now she had a new client — herself.

A FAMILY OUTING IN AFRICA
Charles Hampton and Janie Hampton

A tale of a young family's journey through Central Africa by bus, train, river boat, lorry, wooden bicycle and foot.